OHIO
DOMINICAN
UNIVERSITY™

SINCE 1911

Donated by
Floyd Dickman

THE TINKER'S DAUGHTER

Also by Sheila Hayes

The Carousel Horse
Me and My Mona Lisa Smile
No Autographs, Please
Speaking of Snapdragons
You've Been Away All Summer
Zoe's Gift

THE TINKER'S DAUGHTER

Sheila Hayes

LODESTAR BOOKS

Dutton   New York

Library of Congress Cataloging-in-Publication Data

Hayes, Sheila.
  The tinker's daughter / Sheila Hayes.—1st ed.
    p. cm.
  Summary: Holly wishes that she had a "normal" mother instead of a fugitive from the sixties who runs an antique shop filled with what most people think is junk.
  ISBN 0-525-67497-7 (alk. paper)
  [1. Mothers and daughters—Fiction. 2. Friendship—Fiction.]
I. Title.
PZ7.H314874Ti 1995
[Fic]—dc20
                                                    95-8523
                                                    CIP
                                                    AC

Published in the United States by Lodestar Books,
an affiliate of Dutton Children's Books,
a division of Penguin Books USA Inc.,
375 Hudson Street, New York, New York 10004

Published simultaneously in Canada
by McClelland & Stewart, Toronto

Editor: Rosemary Brosnan   Designer: Marilyn Granald
Printed in the U.S.A.   First Edition
10 9 8 7 6 5 4 3 2 1

to the memory of Nana, who made us all proud

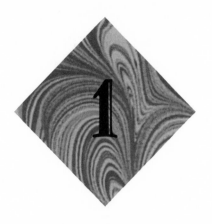

J pressed my forehead against the smudged windowpane of the school bus and wished with all my heart that I could stick my head out the window and ride along like a cocker spaniel, letting the wind whistle through my big floppy ears. Then I wouldn't have to listen to the constant chatter from Kelly Kirby about how wonderful it was to be in junior high school. I looked across the aisle to where Kim Kirby, Kelly's twin, sat immobile and mute. Linda used to say that when they were born, Kelly had grabbed all the words out of Kim's mouth before she could learn how to use them. The weird Kirby twins were one of those things that had never bothered me before Linda left. Of course, they weren't that important back then. They just happened to be Linda's cousins, and you had to tolerate your best friend's cousins. Now the two of them were threatening to become the centerpiece, the linchpin, the whole nine yards of my social life! So I was, I admit, in a pretty morose state that rainy morning, waiting for the moment when we'd stop at Slater and Elm right in front of Linda's house, and I'd stare up at its friendly white porch and look achingly at the wooden swing in the front yard that seemed to sway a little bit in the mornings, as if Linda's ghost was having one last swing before she left.

I shook my head to get rid of the morbid thought. It wasn't as if she was *dead*. No, she'd just been kidnapped. Kidnapped by the Allied Can Company and taken off to Atlanta with the rest of the Wells family. Two weeks before we were to start at the junior/senior high school, seven years after our first meeting in kindergarten. And I wasn't even consulted about the move!

"I can't understand why we haven't spotted her yet," Kelly mumbled a few minutes later, as we swung into the school parking lot.

"Spotted who?" I asked.

"The person that I told you about! It's three days now and there's no sign of her. I can't understand it. I'm sure I'll be able to spot her."

Kelly was hurrying across the lawn ahead of me, and I raced to catch up with her.

"What are you talking about?"

"The famous person who's moving into the condos with her mother. I *told* you."

"No you didn't."

"Yes I did. So now if you want to hear it again," she said primly, "you'll just have to wait until lunch."

There. I'd been a naughty girl and not paid attention, and now I was being punished. *Oh Linda, how could you do this to me?* Kelly Kirby knew that I didn't have anybody else to eat lunch with. I was trapped.

I caught a quick glimpse of myself in the glass doors of the entrance as I raced down the hall to my locker. I have to stop wearing so much black, I realized. When I reached my locker, I ripped the paisley shawl off my shoulders and tossed it onto one of the shelves. Once in a while the shawls came in handy, I admit, to hide a split seam or a stain. And I wouldn't want to hurt my mother's feelings for the world. But sometimes I got so tired of having to smuggle new clothes I'd bought with baby-sitting money into the house, or hiding them in my locker till they looked "used" enough to satisfy her.

Maybe here's where I should back up a bit and introduce myself. In order to understand how dev-astated I was when Linda Wells left town, you really have to know who I am. To be more precise, whose daughter I am.

I am the daughter of Paisley Gerard, she of Pais-ley's Place. She who renamed herself after a shawl somewhere around 1968, when she hung out in Greenwich Village telling fortunes with hair down to her waist and "love beads" around her neck. (I've seen pictures.) She who had found her home in the sixties and never really left, even after she'd come back to live in Old MacIntosh, Vermont. She who runs an antique shop that some have called a junk shop, full of old clothes and "collectibles." She whose biological clock went off with a BOOM when she was thirty-something, resulting in the arrival of *moi*, the joy of her life, on Christmas Day twelve years ago. Father? All my birth certificate says is *unknown*. All Paisley says is *superior genes*.

I love her, but normal she's not, and all my

life—ever since I was old enough to realize what number I'd drawn in that big family lottery in the sky—I've wanted more than anything else in the world to be normal.

Which is where Linda Wells comes in. She got my share of normal. Where my mom is stuck in the sixties, her mom is right out of the fifties. She has two moronic little brothers, a father who says "gosh darn" when he swears, and the kind of house that's filled with ducks. Not real ducks, of course. (That would be more Paisley's style.) But ducks of every color and description on the walls and tables, little ducks holding napkins on the kitchen counter, little ducks holding the soap in the bathroom.

From the time I realized how weird our house was, I preferred Linda's. Ours was the kind of friendship that excluded everybody else, and now I realize that maybe that wasn't too smart. But being Linda's best friend always made me feel just great. It made me feel safe, it made me feel anchored. And when she moved away it made me feel betrayed.

So here I was on the third day of junior high, almost having a nervous breakdown because I was entering the cafeteria alone at lunchtime. As I grabbed a tray and got in line, I took a deep breath, as if self-confidence was in the air like oxygen and you could breathe some of it in if you just tried hard enough. Then I gave everyone in line my "vague" smile. The way it worked was this: If they saw it and smiled back, it counted. But if they looked straight through me—the way they were doing right now—it was no more important than a sneeze.

4

I craned my neck trying to spot either of the Kirby twins as I paid for a tuna fish sandwich, a Devil Dog, and a Coke. I actually agreed with Kelly that junior high was exciting. But God, it was so nerdy to say that! Probably everyone has nerdy thoughts once in a while. But Kelly Kirby just spits them out and hangs them up where everyone can see them!

I made my way across the cafeteria, balancing my tray in front of me while I searched frantically for any sign of them. What if they weren't here yet?

"Holl-ee!"

With a sigh of relief I made my way over to where Kelly was waving and pointing to the empty seat next to her.

"Whew. I was beginning to think I was going to have to stand. This place is a madhouse!" I said.

"Don't worry, we'll always save a seat for you," Kim whispered earnestly. I smiled my phoniest smile, hoping that the proper amount of gratitude shone in my face.

"So," I said, as I unwrapped my sandwich, "what's all this about somebody new?"

"Maybe now we'll just make you guess," Kelly said, "since you didn't pay attention the first time I told you!"

"Oh God, you guys are so queer!"

"I don't think she'll get it in a million years," Kim mumbled, shaking her head.

"Get what?" I asked, beginning to get really annoyed.

"Who this glamorous person is that's moving in and going to go to school right here ... with us!"

"Michelle Pfeiffer."

"Too old. But you're close."

"Michelle Pfeiffer is *close?* I give up. What're you guys talking about?"

Kelly leaned across the table as if she were passing along the answer in an algebra exam. "Massun Brun," she whispered, barely moving her lips.

"What? Who the heck is Massun Brun?"

"Shh! Keep your voice down. No one is supposed to know!"

"Well, your secret is safe with me. I still don't know. Who is Massun Brun? I never heard of him."

"It's not a him, stupid. It's a her." Kelly was using her patient teacher's voice. Then, in a hushed tone: "Madison Brown."

"I still don't get it. Who is she?"

"Boy, are you dumb, Gerard. She's an *actress.* She was on an "ABC Afterschool Special" just a couple of months ago!"

"Oh."

"Is that all you can say?"

"What's the big deal?"

"Well, it's exciting to have somebody new around. But they just want to blend in, keep a low profile. That's what Fleur said. Don't you love it?"

"Who's Fleur?"

"That's her mother. She used to be a Playboy Bunny, I think. That's what my mom says."

"Let me guess. She's been in the store," I said.

"Not exactly, but Mrs. Peterson was, and she lives two doors down from them."

"Good for her."

Although Kirby's was the biggest store in Old MacIntosh, Macy's it wasn't. But to Kelly and Kim, it was the center of the universe. Nobody in town could get married, arrested, divorced, or drunk without every last juicy detail passing over the scanner along with the broccoli and the rhubarb.

"*There she is* . . . I'm sure of it!" Kelly squealed suddenly.

I turned in the direction that Kelly was pointing and saw a girl sitting alone at a table against the wall. Her brown hair was pulled back in a ponytail and she wore large tortoiseshell glasses. All that I could see of the rest of her was a blue denim shirt and a brown belt with a silver buckle.

"She doesn't look like anything special to me," I said, scrunching the sandwich wrapper into a little ball until it crinkled. "I wonder why they moved to our town?"

"I don't know," Kelly said. "But they came here from New York! Can you imagine having this glamorous creature sitting right next to you in class? Maybe she'll want to hang out with us. Give us beauty tips!"

"You're crazy. She doesn't look like a glamorous creature to me."

"Oh yeah? Well that's all *you* know. I heard she had a part in a movie with Kevin Costner!"

"Really?"

"Really."

"Well, then I guess a few tips couldn't hurt," I said.

J guess if I was really sharp (like Kelly Kirby) I would have recognized my new locker mate from the back as I came down the hall the next morning. But being in my usual morning funk I didn't, so what can I tell you? Momentous events in our lives often happen like that, I'm told; no trumpets, no sirens. They sneak up on you and before you know it they just ... happen.

"Oh," she said, as I reached the lockers and realized that this perfect stranger had opened *mine* and was placing things neatly inside. "I'm sorry, is it okay if I take the bottom shelf? No one was here so I just went ahead. Of course, if it's a big deal, I can move everything."

I swallowed hard and tried to be nonchalant, which is like a fish trying to ice-skate.

"Oh, that's fine. I mean, I don't care."

I stood there turned to stone while she organized her things on the locker shelf and everyone around us, including the Kirby twins, stared at us openmouthed and seemed to move in slow motion. Finally she finished and turned to me, adjusting her large, owlish-looking glasses.

8

"I guess we should be introduced if we're sharing a locker. I'm Maddy Brown," she said, giving me a smile that showed off absolutely perfect teeth. The thought that they were false crossed my mind, but then I knew that that was stupid. (I mean, how many twelve-year-olds have false teeth? But for the ten seconds it crossed my mind it made me feel better.)

"I'm Holly Gerard," I said, as the first bell clanged, sending everyone into fast-forward.

"I hope we're going to be friends," she said, as I stretched around her to grab what I needed.

"Sure," I said, pulling off the belt I was wearing and tossing it on top of the gym socks rolled up on the floor of the locker. This morning the belt had seemed fine, but now as I stood next to Madison Brown I knew it was all wrong.

"Could we maybe do lunch? At noon ... in the cafeteria?"

I'd love to be able to say that I recovered my mental faculties enough to answer, "Sure, Maddy! Love to! See you then!" But all I remember doing is nodding dumbly as I raced down the hall with the second bell ringing in my ears.

She got to the lunchroom ahead of me, and as I made my way down the line, I saw her waving to me from the same table against the wall where she'd been sitting yesterday.

The table was small and my part of it seemed crowded (maybe it was the two packs of Twinkies), so I got rid of my tray as soon as I settled in. Then I sat there trying not to let her catch me

9

staring at her. While I undid the cellophane on my sandwich and popped open my soda, I kept stealing glances across the narrow table. She was having yogurt and an apple and the thought hit me that I could never really be friends with someone who ate yogurt and fruit for lunch, but then I remembered about Kevin Costner and shoved the thought out of my mind. She had a really serious look on her face as she arranged everything neatly in front of her and unfolded the small paper napkin. But beyond the seriousness, I decided, she looked really pleased. As if eating in a cafeteria was an exotic thing to do!

"So ... your name is Holly Gerard and your locker number is 767—that's about all I know about you! If we're going to be friends, we have to know a little bit more, don't we?" My face must have registered *blank, no one home*, because she added, "I mean, you don't do drugs or anything, do you? I'm not going to find little packets of white powder squirreled away on the top shelf?" She giggled then, as if that was the most hilarious thing in the world, and for a moment I wanted to point out Billy Richman and Petey Schneider, who'd been sniffing everything sniffable for the last six months. They sat together at an adjoining table, lost in their own private world. But I figured I didn't have to. This was Old MacIntosh, Vermont, but she came from *New York City!*

"No," I said finally. "I don't do drugs or anything."

"Great. Neither do I. And I can't stand kids who do. It's so *stupid.*"

"Where did you go to school before?" I asked, somehow finding my voice.

"Professional Children's School in Manhattan." Then she added, "In New York City?"

"I've heard of that," I said, a hint of defensiveness in my voice. "I've been to New York lots of times."

"Really? Oh good! Then we'll have lots in common. Don't you just love it?"

First test.

My tongue was already around the words "Actually, no" when I checked myself. No need to lie. Just fudge a little, the way Paisley does when someone asks her how old something is. "It definitely has *age*," she always says wisely. I remember one time wanting to yell out to a tourist—who was holding a cracked, stained teapot as if it were a holy relic—"Everything has *age*, stupid! From the minute you're born you have *age*!" But I didn't, and as usual the woman had just smiled and paid for it, and left the shop with the treasure clutched tightly against her Ralph Lauren ski jacket.

"It's an interesting city," I said.

"It's more than interesting," she said. "It's vital, it's alive, it's—" She stopped then, as if some invisible director had just yelled "Cut!" "But this is a *lovely* place. Have you always lived here?" Her eyes grew wide, as if the thought of such a thing was causing some kind of brain strain.

I nodded. "Yeah, I was born here. So was my mother." *Whoops. Don't say anything more! The less she knows about you, the more she'll like you.*

11

"Really? Oh, that's perf ... great."

I watched her spoon the yogurt delicately into her mouth. "Is that all you're having for lunch?"

She nodded. "I have to be careful," she said. "The camera adds pounds and I have a tendency to be chubby."

"You don't look chubby to me." The *camera?* I could feel a rush of adrenalin. Maybe this was the moment to ask her about Kevin Costner. But I decided not to pry. I didn't want to sound like a *groupie.*

"Well, that's because you're not in the business. Not that I'm going to work right now. I have to concentrate on my studies." She rolled her eyes in a way that gave me reason to hope. Maybe she was a moron! That would be so neat—sort of balance the scales.

"My father's already thinking about college. He's hell-bent on my getting into his alma mater."

"And where's that?" I asked politely, as hope gurgled out of me like water from an unplugged fire hydrant.

"Yale," she said.

"Oh." I took a deep breath. "So, what made you move up here?"

She paused, suddenly looking uncomfortable. Had I gone too far? It was an obvious question, wasn't it? I mean, it wasn't like this was Boston or Washington, D. C. People didn't usually move from New York City to Old MacIntosh.

"Can you keep a secret?" she whispered, leaning over the table. *She was in a Witness Protection Program!*

12

No, there weren't many mobsters who went to Yale. She ...
"Holly?"

"Oh ... oh ... of course I can!" I said, nodding vigorously.

"I have to be a *normal teenager* for a while."

"You're researching a role?"

"No, not for a role," she said, sounding a little annoyed because I wasn't getting it. Whatever *it* was. "Holly, you have no idea what it's like to be a professional. I just woke up one day and said, 'Hey, guys, that's it, I've had it. I want to live a nice, normal life, like other kids my age.'"

"But why here? Why did you come all the way up to Old MacIntosh? It's so far away from everything!"

"Well ... actually, we picked Old MacIntosh because it *is* so far away from everything. They won't hound me up here, plead with me to do just one little bitty role."

"You're not going to act anymore?" I said, hearing the disappointment in my voice.

"Of course I will. But, during vacations. Right now, it's really important that I catch up."

"Catch up?"

"That's right. No more auditions, no more photo layouts, no more interviews. I don't expect you to know what I'm talking about. When you've led a nice, normal existence all your life, you can't possibly understand."

Here's where I should have interrupted her, I know. I should have said, "Nice and normal? We're talking major weird here, Madison!" But I couldn't

13

let her know that I'd depended on Linda to make me feel nice and normal, and without her I felt like a big blob that didn't fit in anywhere. No, I couldn't let her know that, because I would lose her then. She would get up and walk away and go find somebody like Jillie Barnes to be friends with. Somebody who was pretty and popular and not having a midlife crisis just as she'd reached puberty.

The hesitation must have shown on my face, because she let out a big sigh.

"Let me guess. You have so many friends already that you're wondering if you can possibly make room for one more, right?"

I looked at her, but if she was making fun of me it didn't show.

"No, that's not it." Should I bare my soul to this girl I'd just met? I agonized for about ten seconds. "Actually, my best friend just moved away. Linda Wells? She was transferred to Atlanta . . ." I swallowed hard. "So, you couldn't have come at a better time."

"Oh, I am so relieved! I just had a feeling—for an actress so much is intuitive, you know?—that you and I would hit it off."

Gradually kids were beginning to clean off their tables, and I began to make a little pile of my lunch wrappings.

"What are you doing?"

"Getting this junk ready to throw away."

"Why don't you just leave it? Oh, don't tell me! I get it. We clean our own tables, right?"

This girl really wasn't kidding about needing to catch up.

"Right. Like in McDonald's, you know?" She nodded unconvincingly. "You *have* been to McDonald's, haven't you?"

"Of course I have! Holly Gerard, you're poking fun at me!"

Every once in a while a southern lilt crept into her voice. "You have a little bit of an accent, do you know that?" I asked.

"Well, aren't you the detective! I was born in New Orleans, but I've been in New York since I was seven. And if my diction coach knew you picked it up, I'd get *killed*." She leaned forward again and giggled.

I felt a flush of pleasure. It was going to work! This was by far the most exciting person to move into town in my whole lifetime. And she had chosen me, Holly Gerard, to be her friend.

"Listen, can you show me where to get some school supplies?" she asked.

"Sure, we can go to Kirby's General Store. You can get almost anything there."

"Great. You don't mind?"

"Of course I don't mind, Madison."

"Oh, please call me Maddy. All my friends do."

"Okay ... Maddy."

"Now, if I'm going to learn what it's like to be you, I've got to learn something about you! You said your mom was born here. What about your dad?"

"Oh, uh, he's dead," I said, crossing my fingers in my lap. (If there is such a thing as becoming a professional liar, I think I'm almost there.)

Now, before you yell at me, think about it: He

could be, couldn't he? I find that dear old Dad changes a lot, depending on my needs at any given moment.

"Oh, I'm sorry. How did it happen?"

I really would have liked to make him a war hero, but I'd tried that before, and it just never seemed to work. "It was an accident ... when I was a baby ... in another city. And they never found the body." (That last touch was in case she decided to go put flowers on his grave.) Most of the kids in town didn't ask; so many were missing fathers anyway. But here was my chance to start clean. To be the person I would like to be.

"Oh, gee, that's awful."

She took it so hard that I had terrible guilt pangs.

"Oh, it's all right," I reassured her. "It happened a long time ago."

"Yeah, but you see, Holly, I need a real old-fashioned family. You know, two parents, two kids. Do you have any sisters or brothers?"

I shook my head. I had no idea what she was talking about, but I could see my fantasies of having an exciting new friend fading quickly.

"Does your mom at least stay home, or does she have a *career?*"

Again I crossed my fingers in my lap. "Oh, no," I said, "she stays at home."

"Well, that's something," she said, as if I had finally gotten an A on some big invisible checklist.

I wasn't really lying. It was true. I just didn't add that home was Paisley's Place. Anyway, you couldn't call what Paisley did a *career.*

16

"Do you have that kind of a family?" I asked tentatively. Maybe it was some kind of religious thing.

"Oh, of course not, there's just Mom and me. Dad left two years ago. But see, *that's* the whole point."

"I'm sorry, Madison, but I don't get it. What's the whole point?"

"I want to do all the things a regular teenager does, live a normal teenage life. But see, I'm going to need a role model for that. And I was so counting on you to be it!"

Kelly and Kim had been trying to get my attention from their table across the way and I'd been ignoring them. Suddenly I had an idea.

"Gee, a real nuclear family—that's what you're talking about, right?" She nodded. "Well, I'll tell you, the only good example that I know of here in Old MacIntosh would be the Kirby twins."

I motioned to where they were sitting and as Madison turned around to look, they started giggling and waving frantically, just as I knew they would. She turned back and I knew from the expression on her face that I was in.

"On second thought, you'll do just fine," she said.

17

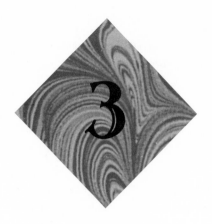

The good thing about my mom having lived in Old MacIntosh most of her life is that everybody knows all about her and all about me and all about how we live up in that apartment behind Paisley's Place.

The bad thing about my mom being a native is all of the above, and I began to live in dread of the moment that Madison Brown would find out that her new best friend was not exactly a charter member of the Brady Bunch.

I am not stupid; somewhere down deep inside I knew that a lie is a terrible, shaky thing to build a friendship on—but what could I do? I figured if we had a little bit of time for the friendship to grow—like maybe four or five years—then I could tell her who her role model really was, and by then we'd be such good friends that it wouldn't matter one bit.

Anyway, that was the plan. I just wanted you to know.

When we hopped off the bus on Main Street after school on Thursday, I took a good hard look at Kirby's General Store, trying to see it through Maddy's eyes. I figured I had to learn to do that, see things the way she did, if we were going to make this friendship work. I sure didn't want her looking at things from where I was at. Anyway, when you first see Kirby's, you might think it's just a country store. That's the idea, actually, the "hook" that lures the tourists who wander down from Manchester when there's no snow to see what a quaint New England town really looks like. Kirby's boasts a sagging front porch and a shingle that blows gently in the breeze with the words *Yard Goods, Produce and Supplies* carved out of a weathered piece of Vermont birch.

The main store is small and cozy and carries fruits and cheese along with newspapers, school supplies, and toiletries. But Kirby's keeps spreading out, and now it's kind of like the Neiman Marcus of Old MacIntosh. There's a clothing "boutique," a dried flower "stall," a furniture "barn," and a gift "emporium," all radiating out like spokes in a wheel from the back of the original Kirby's.

I watched Maddy's face as she slowly walked around inside. Her hands were shoved in the pockets of her jeans as if she might catch some disease if she touched anything.

"Maybe you'd like to see the other shops?" I asked.

"Sure," she said without much enthusiasm.

"I guess it's no Bloomingdale's."

"You can say that again!" she said, with a little laugh. But then, almost as if some teacher had just corrected her and she realized she'd given the wrong answer, she added, "But it's charming, Holly, really charming!" I know it sounds strange, but I was getting the feeling that sometimes she seemed scared that she'd say or do the wrong thing, and for an instant I wanted to say, "It's okay, Maddy, I'll still be your friend even if you don't absolutely love everything in Old MacIntosh!" But I didn't say it, of course, and after browsing around a bit more, she cried out, "Migod, Holly, why are all those *chickens* in there?"

She started toward the entrance to the Gift Emporium and I followed her, confused for a moment. *Chickens?* What was she talking about? Then I knew.

"Those aren't chickens, Maddy, they're ducks," I said.

"I can't believe it! I mean, what *can* they be thinking of?" she said, with that same little laugh that made me uncomfortable, I realized, because it made her sound so much older than me.

I had to admit, seeing them all in one place like this was a bit overwhelming. Maybe it was a family thing; Mrs. Kirby and Mrs. Wells were sisters: Duck love ran in the family.

Maddy walked around the displays, fingering the different items tentatively. She held up a small white duck with a blue kerchief around its neck. Turning it over, she realized its true identity: It was a doorknob.

"Have you ever seen so much tackiness stuffed into such a small space?" she whispered, giggling.

I giggled back, but I didn't really think the

ducks were tacky. The ducks had two qualities I prized above all others: they were *new* and they were *clean*.

"Hi there!"

I recognized the voice, of course, and when I turned around there they were: The only two kids in town that shared a larynx.

"Welcome to Kirby's," Kelly said, with a great big smile, like this was the White House and we were getting to meet the First Lady herself. "May I help you with something?"

Kim stood behind her like a shadow.

"Kelly, it's me. Why are you talking like that?"

"Of course it's you, Holly. And this is Madison Brown. May we call you Maddy?" I had the strange feeling we had stumbled through the Looking Glass. The Queen of Hearts was going to show us around. It was going to be just *ghastly.* "Are you looking for anything special?" Kelly continued, folding her hands in front of her like an old-fashioned schoolmarm. It was the way her mother always stood when she was in the store. Mr. and Mrs. Kirby didn't work there themselves anymore—you wouldn't expect to see Neiman or Marcus behind the counter, would you?—but there were Kirbyisms that were passed down to all the help, and I think Kelly had picked up some of them.

Maddy looked flustered. "Uh ..."

"Maddy was just admiring the ducks. Weren't you?" I said.

Her eyes grew wide.

"Uh, yes. Yes, I certainly was. Especially this little guy," she said, picking up a toilet-tissue holder. "I think maybe I should get this for my mother," she said with a straight face. "She'd love it."

Kelly sighed patiently. "I'm not sure, but I don't think that one comes in the *duck*. Let me just check," and she turned and pivoted away, sort of like Princess Di going off to fetch the footman.

Kim stood staring at the carpet until Kelly returned a moment later, announcing in a voice most people reserve for funerals, "I'm *so* sorry, 2233C does not come in the duck. Only in the piglet."

I saw Maddy glance down, a confused look on her face. The mistake was obvious: Two little pigs, their snouts rising pertly above pink bow ties, stood ready to clutch each side of the toilet paper and see that it rolled out gracefully at the appointed time.

"Oh, uh, maybe I should just let her pick out something herself," Maddy said. "I'm sure she'll be in to see all this very soon."

"I'm afraid the stock is really messed up today," Kelly apologized. "You know how that is, don't you, Holly?"

"Huh?"

"You know how it is when one's shop gets a little bit *messy?*"

I knew it: Kelly was jealous that Madison Brown had picked me for a friend, and now she was trying to ruin everything!

"Uh, yeah," I said, shrugging and moving away from her.

"Holly's family and mine are in the same business, you know," she said to Maddy. "Have you been to her mom's shop?"

But before Maddy could answer I grabbed her arm.

"I want to show you something," I said, adding "Nice seeing you, Kelly," as I shoved Maddy through the Gift Emporium. I didn't stop till we had gone through to the Flower Stall and reached a counter full of potpourri. "Do you like this?" I said, grabbing a bag of Oriental Blossom and shoving it under her nose.

I was only trying to distract her, but it worked so well I almost killed her.

"Yuck!" she said, beginning to gag and choke as she shoved it away. "Don't do that! I'm allergic."

"I'm sorry."

Maddy pretended to be looking at all the different bouquets for a few moments, but she was frowning behind her horn-rimmed glasses as if she was trying to solve some gigantic puzzle. Finally she said, "Your mom has a shop?"

I nodded, my mouth too dry for me to speak.

"Then your mom *does* have a career," she said.

"It's just a little antique business—"

"You told me she stayed at home!"

"She does! She runs the business out of our home."

"Oh."

I could tell the wheels were turning in her head: Did this count as a lie or not?

"Doesn't *your* mother do anything?" I said, trying to knock her off balance so she wouldn't decide to end the friendship before it had really begun.

"Fleur doesn't have a career at the moment," she said, with a touch of frost in her voice. Her mind was going, I could tell. Suddenly she turned back to me and nodded her head like some kind of judge about to deliver a verdict. "You know, that's really good news about your mom. Fleur *loves* antiques. We'll have to stop in. Then I can see your house too!"

"Uh, well, she doesn't let people stop in." A confused look spread across her face, but I forged ahead anyway. "I mean, it's by appointment only." There were dealers who worked that way. They were the really high-priced ones.

"Well then, make an appointment for us!"

"I can't," I said, hoping she wouldn't notice the touch of hysteria in my voice.

"Well, for goodness sakes, Holly, why not?" she asked, in a spoiled-brat tone of voice that I'd never heard before.

"Because"—I let out a huge sigh—"because right now she's in the midst of renovating. But I'll let you know when it's open again, okay?"

"Well, why didn't you say that in the first place? I thought you were trying to fool me or something!"

Fool you? Me?

I was so jittery waiting for Kelly to reappear and drop another bombshell that I heaved a big sigh of relief when Maddy turned to me and demanded, "Holly, where are the school supplies?"

"We passed them when we came in, remember?"

"That was it?"

"That was it," I said.

We returned to the front of the store, where Maddy picked out some notebooks, a package of pens, and two loose-leaf binders. Then we waited in line while Theresa, the town crier of Old Mac-Intosh, held some poor soul captive at the cash register. Theresa was tall and thin, with long black hair parted in the middle and glasses that slipped down her nose a lot while she talked. Some people think Theresa isn't quite right in the head, but my mother says she's just eccentric.

"Eleven pounds, nine ounces. Swear to God. They thought it was twins, but no, just one big lard of a baby. Lord have mercy, that Joanie Williams is such a little bit of a thing she won't be able to walk till the child's in high school!"

"No, no, those aren't mine!" old Mrs. Childs said, getting flustered, as she saw Maddy's loose-leaf binders being swept along with her groceries.

"Well, why didn't you tell me that, Millicent? I can't be a mind reader, can I? Hmm?"

Maddy poked me and we both giggled. To most people it would seem pretty obvious that Mrs. Childs wasn't in the market for school supplies, but I guess not to Theresa.

"Hey there, Holly, how's you doing?" Carefully, Theresa lined up Maddy's purchases in a neat little row, but made no attempt to ring them up.

"Fine, thank you," I said.

She looked at Maddy as if she expected her to

25

speak, but Maddy just stood there, a ten-dollar bill folded in her hand.

"So, how do you like our little town? Not much like Hollywood, I bet, huh?" She looked over our heads to where other customers were lining up. "This little girl's from Hollywood, you know that?"

I could see Maddy's face getting red, and I knew I should do something to rescue her, but I also knew from experience that Theresa would say what she wanted to say no matter what you did, and when she was done, she'd shove the glasses up on her nose and get right back to business. And that's what she did.

"That'll be eight dollars and twenty-seven cents," she announced as she put the supplies in a plastic bag. "You remember to recycle this now, you hear? That's what we do up here."

"I will, thank you," Maddy said, as she took her change.

We were almost out the door to freedom when Theresa called out, "Holly Gerard, you come back here!" I turned around, wondering what she was up to now. Slowly Maddy and I made our way back to the counter. "Almost forgot. Why didn't you remind me? Joe Winslow left this for your mom. Says he don't need it anymore, maybe she can get something for it." And with that Theresa began to rummage beneath the counter. "It's a watering can, I think. Now where did that thing go?" I stood red-faced as she continued to search and the people who'd been in back of us on line began to fidget impatiently. "It's a rusty old thing, but it might fetch a few dollars," she was saying, talking to herself as she straightened up. "Here it is," she said, holding up an ancient piece of tin that most people would toss in the garbage.

"Oh, Theresa, I think you're mistaken. My mother wouldn't be interested in that," I said, and then I turned, leaving Theresa openmouthed, and shoved Maddy out the door ahead of me.

"She's crazy!" Maddy said, as we made our way down the street, giggling. "Can you imagine the expression on your mother's face if you actually brought home that piece of junk?"

"Yeah," I said, so nervous suddenly that I could hardly breathe.

Oh, I could imagine it, all right. Unfortunately, it would probably be an expression of absolute *rapture.*

"*I must have* just missed you in Kirby's today," Paisley said, as she ladled out the bouillabaisse. The smell was terrific and I realized how hungry I was.

"You were in Kirby's?"

"Uh-huh."

"What time?"

"Right after you, from what I heard. About three-thirty." She wiped her hands on her long apron, then smoothed her dark, tangled hair back off her forehead before she sat down. "There. We have everything?"

"Yep," I said, starting to eat.

"So tell me, who is this new friend."

"What new friend?"

"Oh, we're going to be coy? The new friend you were in Kirby's with. How come I haven't heard about her?"

"There's nothing to hear," I said. "She's just a new girl that moved into the condos."

"Uh-huh. Right. She's just an actress—and just from New York. So how come you lied to Theresa

28

and you wouldn't take the watering can? What's going on?"

"I didn't lie to Theresa! How am I supposed to know what you want to stock in this place? That's your business and I'm not ... not a messenger."

"Whoa! Are we going through one of our spells? One of those 'Why can't you be nice and normal like all the other mothers' things?" I decided to concentrate on the bouillabaisse and just ignore her. She liked to talk, Paisley did. To *expound*. It probably came from all that time she spent hanging around the coffeehouses in Greenwich Village. "Haven't you looked around? There are no normal mothers anymore! God, I used to have these flashes of guilt because you didn't have a father. But now I can see how lucky you are compared to other kids. I would hope that you'd appreciate that, too, instead of always moping around the way you do!"

I poised with my spoon halfway to my mouth and shot her a look. Sometimes one *had* to respond.

"Lucky? Now I'm lucky?"

"Look around you, honeybabes! Half your friends have no fathers. Only they suffered—they had to watch their dads pack up and move out. Down the street or out of town or in with the nearest bimbo. Think about it. I spared you that! So now I have to suffer your scorn?"

I know that my mother looks at the world through a fun-house mirror, but still, sometimes her reasoning astonishes me.

"Oh Mom, stop talking like ... like you do. I'm not mad, I'm not ashamed, I'm not moping, all right? Next time I'll take the damn watering can."

"Good. Now when am I going to meet your new friend? She sounds a lot more interesting than that Linda Wells."

"Mom!" She was in one of her moods, I could tell. If I wouldn't argue on one front, she'd go around and try a sneak attack from the rear. "Don't start on Linda, okay?"

"Honeybabes, I'm not starting on Linda. Considering those dreadful parents, she was a sweet, average, uncomplicated child. But this new girl does sound a teeny bit more interesting, you gotta admit that."

I didn't say anything. She was right, of course, but to admit it would be so disloyal to Linda that I couldn't even consider it. Which reminded me.

"Did I get any mail?"

"No. Were you expecting some?"

Of course I was. I hadn't had a letter from Linda in a week. "No," I lied. Then I added, "Not even any catalogs?"

"Oh, you got catalogs. They're around here somewhere. I thought you meant real mail."

I mopped up the last of my stew with a crust of bread and wiped my mouth with my napkin.

"May I be excused?" I asked politely.

"Yes, you may," Paisley answered, just as politely.

For all her strange ways, my mother put enormous importance on manners. I could say *damn* or

30

some other swear word and she wouldn't notice, but if I tried to leave the table without saying "excuse me" I'd be in big trouble. Same thing with "thank you," "please"—all that kind of stuff. I shoved my chair back and then on impulse I went over and gave her a hug. "I love you. And I'm really sorry about the watering can. I'll pick it up tomorrow."

"That's okay, I got it this afternoon. Didn't you notice it?" she said, jumping up excitedly. In a corner of the kitchen, where I can't believe I didn't see it—except of course that the place was so cluttered with junk that I couldn't see *anything*—there was the large, gray, dingy watering can. "Isn't it great?"

"Magnificent," I said.

"You just have no eye, that's your problem."

"Where are the catalogs that came?"

"I don't know. I put them down somewhere. Maybe in the parlor?"

I went into the other room and surveyed what Paisley likes to call the parlor. The overflow from downstairs usually finds its way up here, especially old newspapers and magazines. I guess some of the stuff is interesting, but the novelty wore off for me when I was about six. I let my eyes wander over the debris slowly, the way I had trained myself to do, and sure enough there they were: two new catalogs sitting on top of a stack of *Life* magazines on one of the end tables. I switched on the lamp, moved two stuffed animals and a 1920s sewing kit out of the way, and plopped down at one end of the sofa.

"God, this place is getting crowded," Paisley said, coming in with Pissarro purring in her arms.

"Where's he been?" I asked.

"Just around. I don't ask him where he goes. He's entitled to a private life just like the rest of us."

"But usually if he's out when I get home, no matter where he is, he'll come running over."

"I guess he didn't see you."

It annoyed me the way Pissarro preferred my mother, but to say it would have made me sound as loony as her. I turned the pages slowly.

"See anything you can't live without?"

I shrugged my shoulders, hoping that it wouldn't be too obvious that I was absolutely dying for some of these things. Brand-new—every single thing, brand-new!

"This is nice," I said, flipping the page around so she could see a bright pink crewneck sweater that I would have killed for.

"Mmm. Color's kind of bright, but it's pretty. I think I might have something like it downstairs. Try the row in the back, left-hand table." I didn't say anything and the silence hung between us like a lead curtain. "What's the matter?"

I didn't look up. Whether it was Linda moving out, or Maddy moving in, all of a sudden I felt as if I were going to explode. You ever feel like that? Excited and terrified all at the same time?

"I'm tired of wearing used clothes."

There. I had said it. Nice and polite, calm, not even raising my voice. And I knew it was hopeless;

we had had this conversation a million times before. But somehow it made me feel better—stronger—to say it out loud again.

Paisley let out a huge sigh. "I really can't figure where I went wrong. Holly, you buy something new, it's like—"

"—wearing cardboard. I know, Mom."

"You don't know. Listen, I'm not stopping you. Order something. But we cannot afford an entire new wardrobe. Not with hundreds of perfectly good, expensive, well-made, fashionable clothes hanging on racks downstairs. Clothes that have *lived*. Clothes that have vibrations, personality—"

"Mom. I've heard all this. But I'm tired of wearing stuff that's old enough to be my mother's. No offense, Mom, but I want to go someplace for the first time, and know that it's the first time my sweater's been there too. Can't you understand that? Let me put it this way: I *adore* cardboard. Cardboard is *me*."

Paisley sat there with her spacey look, the one she gets when she doesn't want to face things. She wears it a lot these days. Then I had a sudden burst of inspiration. "I think I need new clothes to impress this girl from New York."

She blinked rapidly and stopped petting Pissarro, who, looking annoyed, leapt off her lap and, after stretching himself like a rubber band, climbed up on the sofa next to me.

"The actress?"

"Yep."

"What's her family like, do you know?"

"There's just her and her mother."

"They didn't happen to live in the Village, did they?"

"I didn't ask, Mom."

I continued flipping through the catalog for a few minutes.

"We should have them to dinner."

I stared at her. "Mom ... come on! How can we have anyone for dinner?" I tried to say it nicely, letting the sentence hang there in thin air, hoping that she would look around her, see things clearly for a moment, and get my meaning.

"Oh, don't worry about this," she said, getting up and beginning to tidy the stacks of magazines on the sideboard. Then she stood for a few minutes adjusting the paisley scarf that hung over the floor lamp. Only when it was at the proper rakish angle did she speak. "After Founder's Day this is all going to be cleared out."

"Founder's Day? What has that got to do with anything?"

"You don't keep up with things, do you? The PTA is sponsoring a flea market, and I'm going to buy a space. I might even take two spaces. We can clean out downstairs, get organized, make a pile of money, and catch up on some bills."

I sat there, too stunned to speak. I had rarely heard my mother sound this motivated to clean the place up. Usually it was agony for her to part with something. That was the problem. She kept buying stuff and hardly ever sold anything. After a while, she'd forget she had bought something to sell it, and it would just become another part of our lives—another part of our lives that needed dusting.

"How did you find out about this flea market?"

Not from the flyer I didn't bring home.

"From Theresa, of course. She knows everything that goes on here."

"When is Founder's Day this year?"

I was playing for time, because the idea of Paisley's Place being on display right on the grounds of the junior/senior high school made me physically ill. Maybe I shouldn't have felt that way, but I did.

"Sometime in October. It's always before Halloween, isn't it?"

"Yeah, usually."

"So, what do you think? I was sure my little sourpuss would be delighted that I was going to get rid of some of this stuff, maybe sprinkle some ducks around."

She bopped me on the head with a pillow and I laughed. She had always made fun of the ducks in Linda's house. I should have told her that Maddy agreed with her. But I didn't.

"I think it's a great idea," I said finally, smiling and not even bothering to cross my fingers.

After all, professional liars don't do that, do they?

"*It's too soon* to work on the float, isn't it?" I said, cradling the phone under my ear.

I was sitting on the floor of my room, putting the finishing touches on my manicure. I always felt when Kelly called me—which she did almost every night now—that if I didn't have something else going on while she was babbling into my ear it was a huge waste of time. Since I'm not really into crocheting, my nails have never looked better.

"It is *not* too soon!" she answered, getting really excited. "Why do you think the seventh or eighth grade never wins? Because they never start early enough! By the time they figure out what's going on, it's too late. The seniors and juniors and all the rest of those guys in the high school start early and end up with these really great floats that always look professional, while the junior high floats always look like the kinds of things we used to make at Camp Kicky Poo." I laughed, and I was impressed. She'd really given this some thought. But then she blew it. "Anyway, that's what Karen told me."

Karen was her older sister. She was in college now, but she was always quoted by both Kirby girls as the sage of all time. I should have known that Kelly hadn't suddenly developed a brain.

"So what are you planning?" I asked, blowing on my nails.

"I think we should have a preliminary meeting. We'll put a notice on the board—a small notice. So they can't say we tried to keep anybody off the planning committee."

"Who's going to be on it?"

"Well, Kim and me, of course. It's our barn."

I must explain that any class project that involved making a mess or hammering nails took place in the old barn on the Kirbys' property. It was just another reason Kelly and Kim thought theirs was the first family of Old MacIntosh.

"And Jillie, of course," she went on. "Which means we have to let Bobby be on it too." Jillie Barnes and Bobby MacCauley have been going together for almost a year. They're inseparable, although the gossip mill has it that there's trouble in paradise since Jillie grew two inches over the summer. But since everyone knows girls get their growth spurt way ahead of boys, I think Jillie's just praying she can keep Bobby interested until he has time to catch up. (By the way, if you are getting the impression that *gossip* is the number-one industry in town—with *rumor* a strong number two—you are absolutely correct.)

Kelly went on talking, adding names to the list. Among the chosen few there was Gina Morrissey, who is very artistic, and Joey Whitelaw, who is absolutely huge and terrific to have around when there is anything heavy to be moved. He also has a great sense of humor and is loved by everyone— including Holly Gerard. When I decide to really fall in love, I think it may be with Joey Whitelaw. But nobody knows that except Linda, and probably she's forgotten by now since I told her when we were in fifth grade.

Finally Kelly got around to asking what I knew she was going to ask, in the way that I knew she was going to ask it.

"So, do you want to be included?"

Kelly liked people to beg. But I had known that since third grade and I was ready for her.

"Ummm, I guess so. As long as it doesn't take up much time."

"Why? What else do you have to do?"

"Well, I have a few other things I'm going to be involved with," I said, knowing that her pea brain was now bouncing around in her head like a pinball, trying to figure out what I could be doing that she didn't already know about.

"Is it Maddy Brown? Is that it? You've certainly become very chummy with her."

"Well, we are very good friends."

"Really?" Is ... is she going to be your *best* friend?"

Ta-da! I had done it! She was broken.

"I'm not sure," I said. But then, as always, I went too far. "But I think she wants to be."

"Did she *say* that? Did Maddy Brown actually say she wanted you for her best friend?"

I got hold of myself just in time. "Not exactly, Kelly. We're just good friends. After all, she didn't know a single soul when she moved here. So I've just been showing her around."

"Have you been to her condo yet? What's it like?"

"Uh, I haven't been there yet," I answered. Kelly couldn't know it, but she had just hit a nerve. Maddy kept hinting that she was dying to see my house, dying to meet my mom, dying to drop by Paisley's Place. But there was no mention of me going to her house, or me meeting her mother.

"Do you think Maddy Brown would like to be on the planning committee?"

"I don't know. Why don't you just ask her?"

"Why don't you? I hardly ever see her. Please?"

"Oh ... okay," I said, with an exaggerated sigh.

"Thanks! So, I'll make up a notice—"

"A small notice," I reminded her.

"Right. And we'll have our first meeting ... when?"

"Next week?"

"Right. Let's see, how's Wednesday?"

"It's okay with me."

"Remember to ask Maddy Brown!"

"I *will*."

"Why don't you call her right now and call me back?"

"No, Kelly, I've got homework to do. I'll ask her tomorrow."

After we hung up, I sat sulking for a few minutes. I couldn't call Maddy Brown *right now* because I didn't have her phone number! It was unlisted, and at first she said she didn't know it and then she said she had to check with Fleur if she was allowed to give it out "for security reasons." If Kelly found out that not only hadn't I ever been to Maddy's house, but I didn't even have her phone number, I don't think she would have worried about us being best friends. Still, there was no one else Maddy seemed to want to hang around with, and even though she sometimes acted bored when we were together, *I* never was. In fact, when I was listening to her talk about her work and all the famous people she knew, those were the only times that I didn't feel left out and miss Linda.

The next morning on the way to school I was thinking about when I'd get a chance to ask Maddy about joining the committee as the school bus screeched to a stop at Slater and Elm. I was glancing up at Linda's window automatically—it had become almost a ritual—when suddenly the front door flew open and a tall blonde girl came leaping down the steps two at a time, yelling "Wait!"

I stared openmouthed. Old MacIntosh was a small town—the kind of town you don't ever have to be lonely in because everybody knows everybody else's business. So it was strange that I hadn't heard that new people were living in Linda's house.

The new girl took the seat right behind Clancy, which was a bold move. But since she was new she couldn't have known the seat behind the driver belonged to Jillie Barnes. Two minutes later when Jillie got on board, she gave her a long, hard look, the kind that would have killed any normal person, but this new girl didn't even blink, and Jillie had to go and sit in the back next to Ronnie Aldrich.

"Who is she?" I asked Kelly.

"Her name is Camilla Moss and they're renting Linda's old house."

"Oh. I didn't even know anybody had moved in."

"It was pretty sudden. Anyway, rumor is she's weird and you won't want to know her, so who cares?"

I was about to ask Kelly to elaborate (notice I didn't need to ask her where she'd heard the rumor), but the bus was swinging into the parking lot so I knew I would have to wait since we all had to make a mad dash to class.

I should explain that I do some of my best thinking in class. For instance today, as soon as Mr. Hill told us to open the earth science book to page 12, I obeyed. Then I sat up straight, folded my arms neatly on the table, picked up a pencil to hold lightly in my right hand, and fixed a look of dazed adoration on him.

That done, my mind immediately got up and left the room.

Today I thought about this new girl, Camilla Moss. The fact that Kelly Kirby thought she was weird was a plus in my opinion. But it did seem strange that somebody else was living in Linda's house. Part of me was jealous because nobody had a right to be living there, and part of me was sad because that somehow meant Linda was really gone and not just away on vacation. But most of all was this feeling that if this new girl was in Linda's house, that made her special. Like maybe fate had sent her to fill up this big hole, which was still there, despite my friendship with Maddy Brown.

At lunchtime I sat with Maddy—as always—which really made Kelly and Kim mad, but I didn't care. A couple of times they had tried to get us to join them, but Maddy had just cut them off with, "Oh, no thank you, Holly and I have a table over here," as if this were a fancy restaurant and the table was reserved. But so far we had always gotten that table, almost as if she had reserved it ahead of time, and I know it drove Kelly crazy.

Maddy usually did most of the talking during lunch, which was fine with me because after that first day she didn't ask me much about myself and that made things a lot easier. She talked about her friends in the Professional Children's School, and about funny things that had happened to her "on the set," and she always had some good gossip that I had never suspected, not even from the tabloids in the supermarket.

But today, when she finally took a break to drink some apple juice—the girl was so health-conscious it was sickening—I jumped right in.

"Guess what! You've been invited to join the float committee."

She gave me a confused look. "The what?"

"Every year in October we have this big event called Founder's Day. They kick it off with a bon-fire on the Sunday night before, then crazy things go on all during Spirit Week, and then on Satur-day everything comes to a head with a parade of floats and a big football game." Here a little chill ran down my back as I added, "And this year there's even going to be a big flea market. Anyway, each grade in the school makes a float to ride around the football field before the big game. And the best float wins."

"Sounds neat," she said. But she said it with that funny little laugh that made me think she meant just the opposite of what she was saying.

"It is, but we have to plan the theme of the float, so we're getting together at the Kirbys' barn on Wednesday afternoon. Will you come?"

She let out a huge sigh. "I guess so."

I was beginning to notice that enthusiasm was not a big part of Maddy Brown's personality.

As we were leaving the cafeteria a few minutes later, the new girl came in through the far doorway.

"See the tall girl by the candy machine?" I said to Maddy.

She looked to where I was pointing, squinting because she wasn't wearing her glasses. "Yeah?"

"She's just moved into Linda's old house. Her name is Camilla Moss."

"Sounds like something growing in a swamp. What about her?"

"Oh, nothing," I said. I guess I was the only one who was a little bit curious. I purposely steered Maddy out that doorway, and as I approached Camilla Moss I let her have it. The "vague" smile. But she did me one better. She immediately dropped her glance and began scanning the ground as if she'd lost a contact lens.

So what. No more significant than a sneeze—right?

43

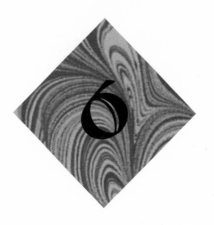

Kelly had taken my advice seriously and tacked up a notice slightly smaller than a postage stamp, so when I took it down on Wednesday afternoon, I really wasn't surprised to see only two names on it. The first name was Danielle Ryan, a small, shy girl who had been a fellow carrot in the second-grade health pageant. The other name gave me a jolt: Camilla Moss. It sure was gutsy, I thought, signing up without being asked. Every time I'd seen her she had been alone. She even ate by herself in the cafeteria. And while that seemed daring, almost adventurous, when Madison Brown had done it, it branded Camilla Moss a loner. And as Kelly had said, "weird."

But now I was having second thoughts about her. Maybe she wanted to make some connection, after all. Why else would she have searched out this tiny piece of paper among all the notices?

"How are we getting to the barn?" Maddy asked on Wednesday morning as we threw our stuff in the locker before class.

"You can go on the bus with the Kirbys and me. You just have to get a pass."

"Oh," she said, clearly disappointed.

"What's the matter?"

"I thought maybe your mom would drive us."

"No, she couldn't drive us. How about yours?"

"Gee, Holly, I never thought to ask. I mean, we're so new here, how would *my* mother ever find her way around?"

I know. This is where I should have informed her that we don't own a car, just a beat-up old van that Paisley uses to haul her junk around and in which I would rather be caught dead than *in*. But of course I didn't.

Horsie was waiting for us when we got off the school bus. For as long as any of us can remember, he's grazed in the field next to the Kirbys' barn. He's old now, but then he's always seemed old. Whenever we go to the barn, we get off right by the fence and he comes over as soon as the school bus stops and rests his big gray head on the fence post, waiting to gobble up the apples we bring him. I remembered to get an apple at lunch today, and now I stood there patiently as he gobbled it out of my hand, stem, pits, and all.

"Aren't you afraid he'll bite?" Maddy said, wrinkling her nose.

"Not Horsie. Especially when you're giving him an apple. He just loves them!"

I stroked his nose and then we continued on up the hill.

Back in the days when Kirby's was really just a country store, the Kirby barn was used for storage. But with all the expansion the store had undergone it wasn't big enough anymore, so now they had a warehouse a mile down the road and the barn had become a great place to have meetings, parties, or sleepovers. But as Linda always said, it had one major disadvantage: It came with Kelly and Kim attached.

Everyone had brought something to eat or drink, and after I had taken a handful of potato chips I passed the bag on to Maddy, who made a face.

"What's the matter?"

"Holly, you didn't even wash your hands!"

"So? What do I have, smallpox? Nobody's washed their hands."

"But not everybody was petting that smelly old horse."

A little shudder went through me, almost like a real quiet alarm bell was going off in my head.

"Horsie is *not* smelly," I said in my most dignified voice. Then I took back my bag of chips, closed it up, and silently hoped that Maddy Brown would starve to death.

After the initial eating frenzy, we settled down on the floor or on packing crates that were stacked against the wall. Even though part of the barn was closed off, the vastness of the space we were in, with its high-beamed ceiling and loft, gave our voices an eerie, hollow sound.

"So ... what's our theme?" Gina asked.

"That's what we're here to find out, dummy," said Bobby MacCauley, and because he looks like Tom Cruise, Gina just giggled.

"Whoops, sorry," she said.

"How about Hawaii?" Jillie Barnes suggested, flashing the smile that made her the prettiest girl in the whole class. Her blonde hair, pulled back in a ponytail, was almost silver, and ever since third grade, Linda and I had wondered if it was bleached. Jillie knows she's adorable, but she tries to act really dumb. I found out it was all an act one morning when her report card slipped out of her notebook as we got off the bus. I almost fainted: all As.

My annoyance at Maddy began to fade, so I loosened my grip on the chips long enough to lean over and whisper in her ear, "Would you believe Jillie went to Hawaii last summer and she's been dying to wear some of the stuff she brought back?"

She smiled stiffly, but I had the feeling she wasn't really comfortable. I guess I should be more tolerant, I thought guiltily. After all, she was new and she really didn't know anybody yet. I'd just never thought about Maddy Brown being socially insecure. I'd always thought that was my own private disease.

"Oh God, Jillie, just because you went to Hawaii . . ."

"Well, I have some leis and lots of other great stuff, and we could all make hula skirts!"

"And freeze our butts off?"

"Good points," she said, giggling.

"How about 'Star Trek'?"

"It's been done."

"That's the trouble, everything's been done!" Jamie Miller said.

47

"As I get it, it shouldn't be just a theme, like Hawaii, but a message, right? I wasn't here last year but I saw pictures, and they had a rocket ship, didn't they?"

The speaker was Camilla Moss and I couldn't have been more surprised if she'd started speaking in tongues.

"Yeah, that was last year's sophomores. It said 'Blast the Bonnerville Bears!' "

"So we're looking for something that will tie in with our opponents, right? Something that would be fun, yet has an undercurrent of aggression about it." She was so *serious* it kind of gave me the willies. But how brave she was, not knowing hardly anybody, to just start speaking right up. Then she made a big mistake. "Who're we playing this year?" she asked.

"I don't believe it—we're planning the float for the Founder's Day football game, and you don't even know who we're playing? Jeez, you been under a rock or something?"

Again the smooth talker was Bobby MacCauley. A lot of the girls call him "Tom" behind his back—which he pretends not to notice—but personally I've never liked him because behind the wavy hair and the dimples lies the personality of a lizard. He continued to torture Camilla Moss. "How can you walk around school all day and not know who we drew for the biggest game of the season?"

"Piedmont Panthers," Joey volunteered, smiling over at Camilla. Then he glared at Bobby, who began to sulk because somebody had spoiled his fun. That's why I liked Joey better than Bobby. Joey might look big and mean like Terminator 2, but behind *his* back, the kids called him "Gumby."

"Thank you," she said. But she didn't offer any more suggestions.

When we took a break to pig out some more, Camilla Moss got up and went over to the table where all the bags and cans were stacked.

"You want something from over there—maybe some Fritos or tortilla chips?" I asked Maddy.

"No ... and don't tell me *you're* going to have more!"

I was taken aback for a minute, as if I'd been sitting next to somebody's mother and hadn't noticed.

"Why not?"

"Because they'll make you fat and give you zits! I know you're not a professional, but you could try just a little bit. See there, you have all those teeny spots around your nose? You really have to be more *aware*, Holly," she said.

"I am *aware*," I said. "I'm aware of the fact that I'm starving to death."

I hope you notice how assertive I was getting. We all draw the line somewhere, they say, and I guess *I* had just drawn it at a bag of tortilla chips. She was always pointing out little grotesque things about me, and maybe these were meant to be beauty tips, but I was getting tired of it.

"Piedmont ... Piedmont Panthers ..." Camilla Moss was talking to herself at the table, repeating "Piedmont, Piedmont Panthers" over and over again, but under her breath so no one could hear her. Except me, of course, because I was sneaking up behind her. Maybe she really *was* some kind of weirdo, I thought.

"Hi," I said. I must have startled her, because she jumped about a mile high in the air. She looked at me a moment, then she frowned, mumbled "Hi" back, and clutching a handful of chips, returned to the corner where she'd been sitting. Gutsy, yes. Friendly, no.

I headed back to where Maddy and I had been sitting with Kelly and Kim, but there'd been a subtle change. Maddy had moved over a few feet, and those few feet made all the difference in the world. She had suddenly found her voice and was talking like mad to Jillie and Joey Whitelaw. Her back was to the twins and, when I sat down, to me as well. I'd been afraid this would happen: Jillie Barnes was much more her speed.

And I bet she wasn't telling *her* she had zits on her nose.

"What do you think of when you think about panthers?" somebody called out as we started up again. The suggestions began to be tossed out.

"Panther ... panther ... pants! We could fill up big baggy pants? Forget it."

"Panther paws. Weren't there some kind of candy bars called panther paws?"

It occurred to me that Kelly was right. It was a good thing we had started early because it was going to take this group a long time to come up with something original. Most of the ideas were really stupid. It also reminded me of how nobody ever really paid any attention to Kelly and Kim. People used the barn, or the store, or anything else they could supply, but they weren't taken seriously. They were always shoved over to the sidelines. Kelly didn't realize that, of course. She and Kim thought they were running things even now, though as usual, they sat by themselves to one side of the room. Correction: They sat by themselves, with Holly Gerard stuck between them like the ham in a ham sandwich.

"How about The Pink Panther?"

The room fell silent for about ten seconds, and then everybody started talking at once.

"Terrific!"

"What a great idea!"

"Why didn't I think of that?"

"That could be a *great* float."

"Where are we going to get a panther costume?"

Gina was off and running. "We'll make one! We get a giant stuffed animal and we put him in pink tights, and a pink turtleneck—"

"We could put the panther in a cute little pink tutu!" Jillie cried.

"With lots of frills and bows. A powder-puff panther for the Mac Maulers to clobber!"

"How about setting his hair—we'll have to have a black wig—in those big pink rollers?"

I turned to Kelly. "Whose idea was it?"

She shrugged her shoulders. "I dunno."

I leaned over to Gina, who was deep into a discussion with Jillie about the merits of pink toilet paper versus pink streamers.

"Whose idea was it?" I asked.

They looked at each other, confused for a moment. "I'm not sure," Jillie said. "I know it wasn't mine. It came from over there. I guess it was that new girl," and she pointed to Camilla Moss.

So she had come up with the theme for this year's float. And she was just sitting there silently, not even grabbing the credit.

I looked at her now and thought how really ordinary looking she was, maybe a little bit fragile even, with shoulder-length blonde hair and bangs and very pale skin. But there was something about her that made me think she'd be a real nice person to know. I don't know why she fascinated me so much, except maybe because she lived in Linda's house. I wondered if she had Linda's room. I wondered if she had brothers or sisters. I wondered about a lot of things. She seemed so incredibly sure of herself. I think that's what I wondered about most of all. Maybe *that's* what Kelly meant when she said she was weird.

When the meeting broke up a little bit later, Maddy suddenly remembered who I was.

"How are we getting home?" she asked.

"Oh, do you need a ride?"

I'd never thought about it! I was hitching a ride with Jamie, who lived just down the road from us, but the condos were on the other side of town.

"Of course I need a ride! I assumed I'd be going home with you. I figured your mom would be picking us up," she said.

"No, I'm getting a ride with Jamie," I said, getting flustered as I realize how annoyed she was.

"So, how am I supposed to get home?" she demanded.

"You need a lift, Maddy?" a voice came from over my shoulder. "I live right near you; my mom'll drop you off."

"Oh, Joey, you just saved my life!" she drawled, sounding suddenly like Scarlett O'Hara.

I know, I know, you're thinking Joey was just being nice again. The trouble is, Gumby doesn't live anywhere *near* the condos.

"*You know* what Bobby calls her?" Jillie said.

"No, what?" Kelly asked breathlessly, as we hopped off the bus behind Camilla Moss.

"Big Bird!" she whispered. "Isn't that *perfect?*"

"*Absolutely!*" Kelly squealed.

Absolutely was suddenly Kelly's favorite word, and I was *absolutely* getting sick of it. Personally, I didn't think the nickname was perfect at all. Big Bird is yellow and tall and *fat,* and Camilla Moss is thin as a rail.

After the meeting at the barn, I did some snooping about Camilla Moss and found out why Kelly doesn't like her. The day she moved in, Mrs. Kirby went over with this little basket she always makes up with samples of jellies from the store (I think they're the ones that are going stale) and Mrs. Moss opened the door and took the basket with just a quick "Thank you," without even inviting Mrs. Kirby inside. I'm surprised she didn't die on the spot. Mrs. Kirby pretends to be real friendly and she does nice, neighborly things like bringing homemade soup over when someone is sick. But then she runs around town telling everybody how messy the sick person's kitchen is, or how badly they need new drapes. Anyway, Kelly's mother managed to get a glimpse inside and said it was the spookiest-looking place she'd ever seen, with bare floors and all the furniture covered with white sheets.

Kelly repeated the story one afternoon to Jillie, Gina, Maddy, and me while we were sitting around putting together some more ideas about the float. They hadn't even asked Camilla to come to the meeting; they said it wasn't "official" and I think that's mean because it was her idea. But I didn't say anything because I was relieved that they'd invited *me*, and I didn't want to say or do anything that might spoil it.

"Everything looked like it had been *bleached*," Kelly was saying, while Kim sat nearby nodding her head in agreement. "Doesn't that sound gross? As if they'd just dipped the whole darn house in a big tub of Clorox. That's what my mom said. She said that must be the way they like to decorate in Pennsylvania."

"Is that where they're from?"

"Yep."

"Well, it doesn't surprise me a bit," Maddy said. Everybody looked at her and held their breath because she was going to give an opinion. "Let's face it, she looks like they dipped her in bleach, too, doesn't she?"

And everybody howled like that was the funniest thing they'd ever heard.

"You'd think her mother would be so grateful that someone like my mother was welcoming them," Kelly continued. "Under the circumstances."

"What circumstances?"

"Oh gosh, I'm sorry. That was a slip of the tongue. I'm not supposed to tell."

"Oh come on, we'll keep the secret!"

"Cross our hearts and hope to die!"

Kelly Kirby ran stubby little hands through her dark curly hair, adjusted the belt on her jeans, and then rolled her eyes heavenward, as if searching for guidance.

"Well, all I can say is, what is the *grossest* thing you can imagine?"

"Give us a hint."

"It has to do with her father. Her *absent* father."

"Oh migod ..."

"He's—"

"A serial killer!" I blurted out.

"Oh, Holly!" Jillie said, laughing.

"Don't laugh," Kelly said, almost in a whisper.

"Her father *is* a serial killer?"

"Not exactly. But close. Now remember, my mother found this out from somebody who works in the office, and this is supposed to be confidential." It was all I could do to stifle a hoot. But for once, she had me hooked.

"So?"

"Her father is ... a *convict!* Right now he's in prison somewhere but he'll be out pretty soon, and then he's coming here!"

"Oh migod, that is *so* disgusting."

"I'd be absolutely terrified to have an ex-convict living in town."

"So would a lot of people, believe me," Kelly said, nodding her head in true Kirby style.

"What'd he do?"

"I don't want to know!"

"Some kind of—what do they call it?—white-collar crime. But my mother said that's just fancy talk for a plain old-fashioned bank robber."

"How awful."

"I'm surprised she can even show her face."

"She figures we don't know, right?"

"Maybe that's why she's so unfriendly," I said, thinking out loud.

"Well, who'd want to be friends with her anyway? I think she knows that, so she's smart enough to not even try," Jillie said.

I decided to forget about Camilla Moss after that because obviously she was a loser, and that *was* a disappointment—to have a loser living in Linda's house with her jailbird father. But I guess there are no real estate laws that prohibit renting a house to people like that. Anyway, I had enough troubles of my own without worrying about Big Bird or Kid Clorox or any of the other names the kids had begun to call her.

My friendship with Maddy Brown continued limping along, with its good days and its bad days.

A typical bad day was the afternoon she'd announced, "Did I tell you that *Seventeen* magazine wanted to do a profile?"

"A profile of *you?*" I asked, unable to hide the awe that had crept into my voice.

"No, a profile of *you*. Of course of *me*, silly! They asked, but my agent told them I was unavailable at the moment."

At times like these I absolutely ached with jealousy of Madison Brown. What must it be like to be so glamorous that a famous magazine wants to write you up and take your picture so people all over the country can know about you!

"They thought I'd be a good role model for kids. That's what they said. You know, how I'm famous and successful but still I manage to be a normal, down-to-earth teenager?"

I wondered how I fit into this picture. I was dying to remind Maddy that *I* was supposed to be *her* role model. This should have made me feel better, more important, you know? But when she said things like, "No a profile of *you*" in that sarcastic way, it made me realize how totally unsuitable it was for us to be friends and got me wondering again why on earth she'd picked me. When we were with the other girls and Maddy and Jillie were giggling together, I would think what a natural pair they made and I would get scared that Maddy would realize her mistake and dump me for Jillie Barnes. But so far it hadn't happened, and most of the time I continued to be grateful, even though there were moments when I thought how conceited she must be to think that she was famous. I mean, I had never even heard about her before she came to Old MacIntosh.

But a *good* day was the Friday afternoon she finally gave me her phone number. "Don't give this to anybody else, promise?" she'd said. We were still lingering at the locker after almost everybody had gone out to the buses.

"I promise," I said. I was the only one in school to have Maddy Brown's unlisted telephone number! It wasn't everything; it wasn't like pricking your finger and taking a blood oath to be friends forever, but for me at that time and place, it was close.

And to top it all off, she said, "Call me tomorrow. My dad may be coming up and I want you to meet him."

So I hope you can imagine how pleased I was feeling a little later as I walked down the hollow from the ridge where the bus leaves me off. I was still feeling pretty good when I noticed a car in the driveway. We don't have that many cars in our driveway anymore. Paisley says it's the economy, but I'm not so sure. Most of the time she just packs up the van and goes off to sell things in other towns, at flea markets and fairs. And when she does she always says she feels like a tinker, and she loves the feeling. Tinkers were gypsies in Europe, where my grandparents came from, and my mother says she would have loved to be one of them, driving around in a wagon with bells on it that tinkled to let people know she was coming. I remember after the first time she said that I had waited for weeks, holding my breath every time she drove the van home, afraid she might have added some bells to its battered exterior to complete the picture. But she never did.

Today the car in the driveway was an old beige Chevrolet, two-toned and very unremarkable, until I saw the license plate. It was blue and yellow with PENNSYLVANIA written across the top, and at the bottom the ominous message: YOU HAVE A FRIEND.

Maybe it was just a coincidence.

I went up the back stairs, trying to be quiet, but it wasn't any use. I heard the door open and Paisley called up, "Holly, is that you, honey? Come on down a minute!"

I don't want to. Oh, how I don't want to. If it's not them, why does she want me to come down? If it is them, I will die. Then I thought how much worse it would be if it was Maddy Brown and her mother. But of course Fleur Brown wouldn't be caught dead in an old place at the end of the hollow. And probably neither would Camilla's mother.

But when I went downstairs, there they were. Mrs. Moss was small and plain, and stood in the middle of the shop looking bewildered, as if to move would mean to be swallowed up in the quicksand of tables, chairs, rugs, clothes, jewelry, lamps, but most of all, dust and dirt that made up Paisley's Place.

"Here she is!" my mother cried. "Holly, these are the people who rented Linda's house!"

Like I don't know.

"Hi," I said. And as I said it, I ducked my head down under the eave and caught a glimpse of

Camilla Moss standing off by herself a few feet away.

Mrs. Moss smiled a small, nervous smile.

"So, is ten o'clock okay?" my mother was saying.

"That'll be fine," Mrs. Moss said. "Sure you can manage?"

"No problem. Holly will help me."

I stared at my mother, but anything I thought to say couldn't be said in front of strangers. While the grown-ups were talking, Camilla Moss stood winding a piece of blonde hair around her finger and staring at me with this blank look on her face, as if I had an old mirror hanging around my neck and she was trying to get a good look at herself.

When they had left, I scrambled up the stairs after Paisley.

"Mom, what was that all about?"

"Those are the people who have rented Linda's house. I thought you knew her—she's in your class. They bought a table and two chairs and a desk lamp. Kind of strange taste, but at least they don't decorate with ducks!"

"I'm *not* going over there tomorrow," I interrupted.

"Why not?"

"Because Maddy's father is probably coming up and she wants me to meet him," I said, trying not to let the pride I was feeling leap all over the room.

Paisley just stood staring at me the way she did sometimes, not asking or telling me anything, making me be the next one to speak. I hated it when she did that.

"And?" she finally prompted.

"And besides, I just don't want to go. It's *Linda's* house—"

"Not anymore. Right now these people are the tenants."

"And they're . . . weird."

"Whoa. Isn't that the pot calling the kettle black?"

My face flushed. "What's that supposed to mean?"

"I mean, lots of people think we're weird. In a town like this, it's a compliment to be considered weird. You should know that by now, or have I failed somewhere?" she said, laughing as she flitted around the cluttered kitchen, wiping off utensils and throwing some pasta on to boil.

"But the kids make fun of her."

"Like how?"

"Kelly's mom went over there—you know how she brings that stuff over?" Paisley rolled her eyes and I went on. "And she told the twins that the place looked *bleached*—as if they had dipped the whole place in Clorox. Only I don't know how she could know that, because Mrs. Moss didn't even invite her in."

"That must have killed old Mary Jane!" my mother said, laughing.

Then I laughed too, feeling better somehow.

"But that's not the worst. Paisley, Mr. Moss is a *convict.*"

"Oh, for God's sake. He got mixed up in that whole savings and loan business."

"You *knew* and you still let them in here?"

"Holly, it's not like he's a serial killer! And who called him a convict? As if I didn't know."

"Well, anyway, I still don't want to go over there. As far as I'm concerned, it's still Linda's house."

"You want it to be a *shrine?*"

"You don't understand. You don't ever understand!"

Dinner was pretty tense, but afterward we made a bet that I thought took me off the hook: I would help her bring the stuff Mrs. Moss had bought over to their house *if* Maddy didn't want me to come over to *her* house. I figured it was a deal made in heaven.

I waited until after nine o'clock the next morning before I dialed Maddy's number. I had carefully rehearsed what I would say if I got her mother on the phone, trying to hit just the right mixture of respectfulness and friendliness.

"Hullo."

"Hello, Maddy?"

"Yeah?" she answered in a muffled voice.

"Did I wake you up?"

"Who *is* this?"

"Oh. I'm sorry. It's Holly." There was a pause that seemed endless. "Holly *Gerard*," I said, swallowing my last bit of pride.

"Oh, oh, right," she said, letting out a big sigh. "Sorry. I didn't recognize your voice. I guess I'm not awake yet."

"Oh, I guess I called too early."

"What time is it?"

"Ten after nine."

"No, that's okay."

There was silence, and I realized I was expecting the happy, chirpy sound of Linda's chatter. Or even the kind of babbling that always streaked through the phone when Kelly called. But there was nothing, except the sound of Maddy Brown breathing. Had she gone back to sleep?

"Maddy?"

"Yeah?"

"You asked me to call, remember? It's Saturday," I added lamely.

"Oh, that's right. I told you maybe we'd ... No, I'm sorry, Holly, he's not coming up after all."

"Oh. I guess you're disappointed."

"Yeah, right."

"Well, we can still do something. You want to take the bus over to the mall in Turner?"

"I don't think so. Actually Fleur has some things she wants to do. But thanks for calling."

"Okay. See you on Monday?"

"Sure. See you on Monday."

The first thing I thought about after I hung up was that now I knew how a guy must feel when he calls for a date and he's slam-dunked. But she *had* given me her phone number. So probably she was just bummed about her father not coming and that's why she sounded so pissed.

The second thing I thought about was that I had just lost a bet.

I knew it was going to be eerie walking in the front door of 14 Slater Drive. I expected to be flooded with memories and I wasn't sure if that would be bad or good, but my first impression was that there was nothing at all here to remind me of Linda and her family. Right away I knew what Mrs. Kirby had been talking about (although I hated to agree with her about anything): The scene that greeted us as Camilla ushered us into her living room did look *bleached.* Not all the furniture was covered with sheets—just two chairs and a sofa. But some of the other pieces looked as if maybe being covered by a sheet was a good idea. Everything had a strange, weathered look about it, as if it was very old or had been left out in the sun too long, and there were lots of clay pots and hanging blankets and brass plates. It looked a bit like someplace out in the desert, or maybe a bazaar in Persia. I was surprised; Mrs. Moss didn't look a bit like my mother but they might have a lot in common.

As Camilla closed the front door behind us, she

motioned to a younger, chunkier version of herself who was just coming downstairs.

"This is Nancy. Nance, this is Mrs. Gerard, and this is Holly."

"Hi!" Paisley said with a big grin.

Nancy's lower lip protruded a bit and she shot a furtive glance in our direction. I think maybe she was struck dumb by Paisley's working duds—biker boots, patched jeans, and a serape—because she didn't say a word but turned and fastened her attention on me, the biker's daughter, giving me the worst look I've ever gotten in my life. You know in the movies where the kid is really the devil and can kill you just by looking at you? Well, that was Nancy.

Before I could manage to stare back, Mrs. Moss appeared from the kitchen, looking flustered as she wiped her hands on her apron.

"Oh, I'm sorry," she said quickly to my mother. "I didn't hear you come in."

"That's okay," Paisley said. "Just tell us where you want the stuff."

"Oh, don't bother them. I can help you bring it in," she said. Then to Camilla, "Why don't you show Holly your room, dear?"

Mothers must take queer pills the moment you're born, I thought. I could tell Camilla was embarrassed.

"You want to see my room?" she asked, rolling her eyes.

"Sure," I said.

Actually, I had been dying to see if she had

Linda's old room, even though I was sure it would look just awful with this strange new girl living in it. I followed her up the staircase with its black railing—at last, something that looked familiar!—then down the hall to the last door on the right—the door to Linda's room.

Then Camilla Moss did a strange thing: She opened it with a key, and after we went inside, she closed the door behind me and locked it again.

But the room wasn't nearly as bad as I had imagined. In fact, my first impression was that here was the real Camilla Moss and right away I got a good feeling, as if the rest was all a mirage and I had been right in the beginning: This was the bedroom of someone I would like for a friend. It was almost—and I know this is really dumb—as if some of Linda had stayed on in the room, like air freshener, just to make me feel comfortable and at home there.

It was a very neat room, but I like things to be neat, so that was fine with me. And Linda's wallpaper was still there: the little pink and white flowers on a gray background. I remember the day it went up and how excited she was because she was getting her room done over for her eleventh birthday. I guess that's why it still looked so good; that was only a year and a half ago. The bookcases that had been built into the wall were still there, too, only now there weren't any kid things like dolls or stuffed animals on the shelves. There were just books and trophies and medals. I went over and looked at some of them.

FIRST PLACE, CENTERVILLE DEBATING TEAM

FIRST PLACE, CENTERVILLE YOUTH GROUP GLEE CLUB

CENTERVILLE MANOR SCHOOL, YOUNG PERSON
ACHIEVEMENT AWARD

SECOND PLACE, CENTERVILLE ORATORICAL SOCIETY

"Don't look at those," she said.

I turned around. She was sitting on the bed, with her hands folded in her lap.

"I guess you must be Miss Superachiever, right?" But that came out sounding a little bit sarcastic and I didn't mean it to, so I quickly added, "Is Centerville where you lived before?"

She nodded. "Uh-huh."

"That's in Pennsylvania, right?" She just nodded again. "So how do you like it here?"

"It's okay, I guess."

"That sounds like you don't like it very much."

She let out a big sigh and just stared at me for a moment. Then finally she said, "Why'd you come over with your mom?"

"I don't know ..." I stammered, suddenly caught off guard.

"Well I do. It was so you could collect some more gossip for your friends."

"I do not gossip with my friends," I said, realizing as I said it what a total, bold-faced whopper I was telling.

She rolled her eyes. "I'll bet."

"Why are you so unfriendly?"

"Look who's talking."

"Wait a minute! I've said 'Hello' plenty of times."

"*Once.* When we were getting potato chips. But after your friends told you about me you stopped saying 'Hello.'"

I rummaged through my memory and realized that it was probably true. I had also smiled at her that first day in the lunchroom, but maybe that didn't count.

"I just didn't think you wanted to be friendly. I mean, you could have said 'Hello' yourself."

"Maybe I didn't want to. Maybe *I'm* not so desperate for a friend that I'd put up with someone like Madison Brown."

"Well, that's all *you* know. For your information, she's not only a ... a swell person and a wonderful friend, but she's also a famous actress!"

"I never heard of her."

"She was in a movie with *Kevin Costner!*"

Her forehead got a little crease in it like she was thinking real hard and I just knew she was impressed, even though she'd never admit it.

"Really? Which movie—what was the name of it?"

"Oh ... uh, I don't know." I never *had* gotten around to asking her about that and now I wanted to kick myself. "What I mean is, I *knew,* but I've forgotten."

"Yeah, right. You're her best friend and you don't know the name of the movie."

"Actually, we're not *best* friends." I should have been flattered that she'd gotten that impression, but instead I found myself stuttering an explanation. "I mean, we've only been friends for a little while because she's new in town. And we share a locker."

69

She didn't say anything and I don't know why, but suddenly I felt compelled to go on and tell this total stranger my life story. "My *real* best friend was the girl who used to live in this house—Linda Wells? In fact, this was her room."

She glanced up at me then. But "Oh" was all she said and then there was a really awkward silence for a few minutes.

"I guess I'd better get back downstairs."

But she didn't get up to let me out. She just sat there looking kind of bummed for a few more minutes.

Finally she said, "Okay, if you want."

But she still didn't move.

"You have to let me out, remember?"

She looked at me for what seemed like a long time but was probably no more than a minute, then got up from the bed and opened the door.

"It wasn't locked."

I stared at her. "What do you mean it wasn't locked? Then what's with the key?"

She shook her head as if she were the teacher and I was being dismissed. "You wouldn't understand."

"Try me."

She let out a big sigh. "It makes me feel better to pretend it's locked. Like I can keep Nance out."

"Why do you want to keep her out?" I know that probably sounds naive, but since I've never had any sisters or brothers, it seems like it would be kind of neat to have another kid in the house to come into your room once in a while.

"She messes up my things."

"Oh, I know. Linda's little brothers used to do that."

"No, I don't think you know. Nance is not your average pesky kid sister. She has major problems."

I thought of the scary way she stared at me downstairs and I believed her. But all I said was, "Oh," hoping I showed the right amount of concern without her thinking I was being nosy.

"It's called acting out."

"Acting out?"

"That's what the shrink says. It's because of, you know ..."

"What?"

"You know ... my father not being here." I just stood there, unable to think of a single thing to say. "You *know* about my father. So don't pretend you don't!"

I swallowed hard. "Okay, so I know. So what?"

"So now you can go and give them the latest juicy morsel: Tell them I pretend to lock my door because my little sister acts like a nut because Dad's in the slammer."

"The *slammer?*"

She stared at me with this really tough look on her face, and for some stupid reason that made me want to laugh. But while I was fighting the urge, *she* started to laugh.

"I figure if I'm going to be a jailbird's daughter I should get to know the lingo, right?"

"Stop it!" I said, giggling. We were both standing near the door now, but suddenly I wasn't anxious to leave. "I'm sure your father's really a very nice person," I said.

She made a face. "He is. But he's also stupid. He trusted some people he shouldn't have trusted. And in the eyes of the law, that makes him as guilty as they are. Anyway," she said, tossing her head, "that's him and it's not me, and if I could only convince the rest of this family of that, life would be much simpler."

"What d'you mean?"

"I mean, I'm not carrying him around with me, okay? Bad enough my mom is and Nance is. I've got my own screwing up to do."

I nodded as if I knew what she was talking about. "Right," I said.

I left the room then without saying another word and started down the stairs, but then I realized she wasn't following me so I turned and went back up a few steps.

"Camilla?"

She poked her head out the door and gave me that look that I used to think was so unfriendly.

"Yeah?"

"I'm not gonna tell them about Nancy—or about anything."

"You sure?"

"Honest."

"Well ... then, thanks."

"You going to the bonfire tomorrow night?"

She didn't answer me right away; there was a pause, as if she was considering it.

"I wasn't planning to," she said finally.

72

"Why not? You should go! It's really neat."

"You going to be there?"

"Sure!"

"Well . . . then, maybe I'll go."

"Good. So I'll see you there, Camilla," I said, and then I hurried out to the driveway where Paisley was waiting.

As I climbed into the van, so preoccupied with what Camilla had told me that I didn't even remember to brush off the seat before I got in, I made a promise to myself: I *wouldn't* tell anyone. No matter how many points I might score with Jillie or Maddy. Or how much I would like to one-up Kelly Kirby, the gossip queen. I was pretty firm in my resolve and I felt good about that.

But then I began to think about the bonfire tomorrow night. What came over me that I urged Camilla to go? What had I said, exactly? What if she expected me to be her friend once she got there? No, I told myself, there's no way she could've gotten that idea. Besides, at night it was dark. You couldn't even *see* people at the bonfire most of the time. You could never find somebody even when you had made elaborate plans to meet them there!

That night I dreamt I was at the bonfire wrapped in one of Paisley's shawls. But I had worn it so that it covered not just my shoulders but my head, my chin, my nose. . . .

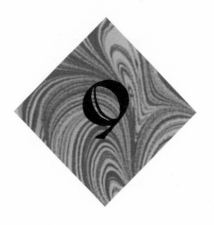

The night was chilly but crystal clear, a perfect night for the bonfire. It always seemed kind of spooky—although I never admitted that to anyone but Linda—to run up the hill in the inky blackness, with only the stars and the torches to light the way. Now, as Kelly, Kim, and I reached the top of the hill and began to inch our way down toward the crowd, we could see the outline of a tower of wood as tall as a building. People would save something in their garage or their cellar all year long just to pile it on the Old MacIntosh bonfire. There was everything you could imagine: broken desks and chairs, bookcases, broken-off tree limbs, and even fence posts.

I *really* missed Linda tonight. We had always carpooled to the bonfire with her cousins, but then Linda and I would lose them in the crowd and go and sit by ourselves on the side of the hill to watch. Tonight I had counted on Maddy being here, but when I asked her, all she said was, "I can't go," and didn't tell me why. So there I was, stumbling downhill in the dark and trying to keep sight of Kelly or Kim and not trip over anybody, when I heard my name being called.

I stopped and squinted into the darkness, across a sea of people hunched up on blankets, and tried to make out who it was.

I heard the voice again, more insistent this time. "Holly! Over here!"

It was Camilla, waving at me as if she'd been waiting for hours. I was so frantic at that moment that I looked around feverishly, hoping to grab onto one of the twins. But they'd been swallowed up in the crowd. So I just stood there not knowing what to do when suddenly—not two feet away from me—I saw Jillie Barnes, Bobby MacCauley, Joey Whitelaw—and Maddy Brown. Maddy glanced up at that moment and, when she saw me, said, "Hi, Holly," as if it were the most normal thing in the world for her to be sitting there when she had told me this afternoon that she couldn't come.

"I thought you couldn't come!" I blurted out before I had a chance to think about it.

"Well, I couldn't until Joey called and offered me a ride."

Double whammy. I had failed her because I didn't offer to pick her up, and I was no longer the only one to have her unlisted number—if I ever *had* been.

I hurried past so they couldn't think I wanted to join them and flopped down on the grass next to Camilla.

"Hello," I said.

"Hi!"

I realized what was making me miserable was probably making Camilla feel a whole lot better. Now she wasn't sitting like a leper, all alone except for the demon sister, Nance, who was sitting on her other side. I searched the crowd but Kelly and Kim seemed to have vanished, so I resigned myself to sitting with Camilla Moss at least for a little bit. She had brought a big Indian blanket, and I stifled the urge to crawl under it and just hide for the rest of the night.

"I thought maybe you weren't coming. You're so late!" she said.

"Well, Mrs. Kirby was late picking me up."

I don't have to sit with you, you know. I didn't promise!

"I can't believe that pile of wood! Is it always that huge?"

"Oh, yeah. I've been coming here since I was well, like Nancy, and it just gets bigger every year."

At the sound of her name, Nancy's head shot forward like a snake's, and she hurled me one of her looks. Then she sank back again so I couldn't see her. I rolled my eyes at Camilla.

"How would you like to live with that?" she whispered out of the side of her mouth.

I didn't intend to laugh, but I did, the giggling releasing some of the tension.

"I guess it's not nice to laugh," I said, suddenly overwhelmed with guilt. "I mean, she's still little."

"You're right. But if I didn't laugh," she whispered, "I'd kill her."

I poked my head out again and decided to try

and make friends. "So, Nancy, what grade are you in?"

Again the look. I glanced at Camilla in the dark, searching her face for a clue. "Now what'd I do?"

"She was *left back*," she mouthed.

"Oh," was all I could think of to say.

"Are you riding on the float on Saturday?" Camilla asked, changing the subject.

"Actually, yes, I am."

"I thought you would be," she said, nodding.

I didn't tell her that this was one of the times that being friends with the Kirbys had paid off. Since it was their truck and the float was being built on their property, not only did they get to ride along with kids like Jillie and Bobby, but they could pull somebody like me on board with them.

"We're getting together at our place to put the float together on Saturday morning before the game," Kelly had announced the other day. "Now, it's going to be Jillie and Bobby, Maddy and Joey, Jamie, Gina, and Kim and me, of course, and then I told them that I thought you should be included. That way you'll get to ride on it. You know how it is, if you don't actually take part in the building, you don't always get to ride. They thought it might be too crowded, but I insisted," she added.

I don't know what upset me more: the deliberate way she had to let me know that I wasn't really wanted on the float, or the way everyone automatically made a couple out of Maddy and Joey these days.

I didn't want to admit all this to Camilla, of course, but I felt the need to explain.

"The only reason I'll be on the float," I said, "is because I've known the Kirbys forever. Linda Wells, remember I told you she was my best friend?" She nodded to let me know she remembered. "She was their cousin."

"Oh," she said, wrinkling her forehead a little. I knew right away what she was thinking.

"But she wasn't like them at all!"

"Thank God!" she said, and again we laughed.

Then all attempts at conversation halted as the chanting started below. It surged around us, sweeping us up in a gigantic wave of sound. Despite the fact that I still wanted to kill Maddy Brown for several reasons (one of which had his arm around her at this very moment), I felt great being a part of the excitement.

And then suddenly the fire was lit. It began to crackle and there were popping noises, and for the first time I noticed the fire truck that always stands over to the side under the trees and the volunteer firemen standing around the perimeter of the fire to make sure nobody gets too close.

And then it all went up in smoke—if you'll excuse the pun.

"Hol-lee!" The scream pierced the night air, cutting through the chanting and the laughing and stabbing the fun right out of me. I looked down and Kelly was standing there, her hands on her hips like somebody's mother. "Hol-lee," she repeated at the top of her lungs, "what are you doing?"

"Kelly?" I called back softly, hoping the note of puzzlement in my voice would let everyone know I was totally bewildered by this screeching person who was waving her arms frantically over her head, like someone flagging in a 747.

"We've been looking for you! You know we're supposed to stay together!"

That was the rule in the fifth grade!

"I'll be there in a minute," I yelled, hoping that the fire and the screaming and the general chaos would mute the disgrace of being summoned like a two-year-old.

"Sorry," I said to Camilla. "I gotta go."

"That's okay," she said. But I could tell she was disappointed, and I felt a fleeting pang of guilt.

I pushed my way through the crowd and felt the heat of the fire as I got closer to the ground. When I reached them, Kelly had her arms folded. All she needed was a tapping foot and she would be the perfect homeroom monitor.

"What is your problem, Kelly Kirby?"

"*My* problem? You were supposed to be with *us*, remember?" Kim just stood there giggling.

"Well, you disappeared and Camilla asked me to sit with her for a minute."

"God, how could you?" It was Gina, who was standing near the fence.

"What do you mean, how could I?"

"You know what I mean," she said. "Now that I know about her family I don't want to have anything to do with her."

"Oh for God's sake, Gina."

"I'm sorry, but like my mother says, the apple doesn't fall far from the tree. Just be sure you watch your lunch money if you're going to pal around with her."

"Oh Gina, that's so stupid and unfair! You can't blame her for what her father did!"

It was very subtle, which was unusual for a Kirby, but I saw it anyway: Kelly rolled her eyes and pursed her lips at Gina, and then she said, "You're right, Holly."

"What was that all about?" I asked, as we hunkered down to watch the last of the blaze.

"What was what all about?"

"The face you made at Gina."

"You're imagining things."

"I am not!"

"Listen, Holly, don't yell at me just because I'm trying to be nice, okay?"

"Nice? What's *nice* got to do with it?"

"I mean, I know you must feel sympathy for Camilla Moss. You also have an ... *unusual* situation. Not that your mom is a criminal or anything! But you gotta understand that we make an exception in your case because we've known you all our lives. My dad says he remembers your mom when they were in school together and she was almost a normal person. So it's different. It isn't just that Camilla Moss has a weird family, she's a *stranger*. So anyway, don't be so defensive, okay? You can relax. We'll always accept you, even *without* Linda. I just wanted you to know."

The fire was beginning to burn down and now

the football cheers were starting in earnest, mercifully drowning out anything further she might have said and making it impossible for me to try and answer her.

> We are the MAULERS from Mac-Intosh!
> We cherish vict-ory!
> Although we're small
> We stand up tall.
> We can-not stand to lose, oh no!
> Go! Go! Go! Go!
> Go ... Mac MAULERS!!

I knew that Kelly, even though she had that twisted Kirby way of doing things, honestly thought she was making me feel better. And what she said should have put my fears to rest; maybe I *didn't* need Maddy Brown to be "in."

I thought about it while we watched the last embers sizzle and die under the firemen's hoses. And I thought about it all the way home.

I should have been feeling relieved, relaxed, happy, even.

Why *wasn't* I?

"*Did you see* my father's letter in the newspaper?" Kelly asked as we made our way to math class one morning.

"No, I didn't," I said.

"I don't know how you could have missed it. It was the first one on the 'Letters to the Editor' page."

"Why would I read the letters to the editor? They never have anything to do with us."

"Well, this time they did. They're going to have a hearing of the planning board Thursday night on whether they should allow Mrs. Moss to sell things out of their house. Can you imagine the nerve? It would establish a very bad *precedent* if they did."

Kelly loved to show off all the big words she knew. I was going to call her on it, because I was pretty sure she was just parroting her father and didn't have any idea what "precedent" meant, but I didn't because I was more upset about what she was saying.

"But why would they try and stop her? My mom runs a shop in our house."

"But that's different. Your mom was *born* here. And the zoning over where you are is different. Can you imagine a store on Slater, right where the bus stops? No, they won't just *try* to stop her, they *will* stop her. You know she's just a front. As soon as *he's* out of prison, whammo, he'll take over!"

"Kelly, they have to make a living, don't they?"

"Not here they don't! You want this place to become a haven for criminals? You want every ex-con within a hundred miles pouring into town when they get paroled? It won't be safe to walk the streets!" I was pretty sure *that* was Mary Jane Kirby talking.

"I think you're exaggerating, Kelly. But anyway, there's nothing you can do about it. That's for the planning board to decide."

"There certainly is something every one of us can do about it. We can go to the meeting Thursday night."

"Oh come on! Kids don't go to those."

"Yes they do. Remember when they were thinking of opening up a teen center?"

"Yeah."

"And all the kids went with a petition?"

"Right, and we still don't have a teen center."

"But you never know. This Thursday, they might bring it up again. So we can go like *that's* what we're really interested in, but we'll really be there to lend support when they talk against this other thing."

"But why would we want to do that?"

"Because. If she doesn't get approved, then

they'll move and somebody we *like* will move into Linda's house. So anyway, everybody in town's got to come. Even your mother."

"Oh, I don't think so. My mother doesn't like to get involved in local politics," I said, crossing my fingers.

"Well, she should get involved this time. She's well ... sort of a merchant, and I'm sure she wouldn't want the competition. Mrs. Moss wants to open a shop selling things from foreign countries. My father said it would be just awful for the town's image when it gets around who they really are. Can you imagine? Any money you'd give them would probably fly right out of the country to ... to terrorists. You really *should* have read his letter, Holly. I'll try and get you a copy."

"Would you really?" I said. "That would be neat."

As soon as I got home that afternoon I asked Paisley if she'd seen Mr. Kirby's letter in yesterday's paper.

"Sure did," she muttered.

"Is it still around?"

"Yep," she answered.

"So, can I see it?" I asked, knowing it would probably take me days to find it among the stacks of newspapers.

"It's right there," she said, and she motioned over to the corner of the kitchen reserved for the cat.

"What?"

"I used it to line the litter box."

"But you *never* clean the litter box. It has to

smell like a toilet before you notice, and then you make *me* do it. All of a sudden you got the urge?"

"It was the only thing I could think to do as a form of protest." When Paisley said the word *protest* my scalp began to tingle. "The man's a fascist," she added, in case I'd missed the point.

"It couldn't be that bad," I said.

"Oh no? You didn't read the letter!"

"How could I? You let Pissarro pee all over it!"

Ignoring me, she went on. "This time the Kirbys have gone too far! You know how I hate those board meetings, but I may have to go to this one. Persecuting that nice woman."

"Paisley, you know you don't want to go to the meeting."

"What do you mean, I *don't want* to go? It's not a question of what I *want*. You should go too. We can't let the Kirbys take over this town. They're ruining it. First all those damn ducks, now this."

She went on like that for half an hour while I finished my dinner and went off to do my homework.

It was really very simple, I decided. If my mother went to the meeting, *I* would not. Absolutely not. No way.

Even though it was a rainy night, by the time we got there the meeting was already so crowded that we had to search hard to find two seats together near the back. Paisley had dressed in basic gypsy for the occasion: A long, black wool sweater (which had gotten wet so it had that real nice *wet wool* smell) over a long, green chiffon skirt that was tucked into the waist on one side to show off the red plaid skirt she was wearing underneath. She wore Afghanistan beads around her neck and not one, but *two* paisley shawls wrapped crisscross over her shoulders. The only thing that kept me from coming thoroughly unglued was the fact that Maddy Brown wouldn't be there. She said her mother had no interest in village doings; I guess it had something to do with living in the condos.

At first I didn't see anyone we knew and I began to breathe easier. But as we settled ourselves and the meeting began, I had a chance to look around and, sure enough, there in the front row on one side of the aisle sat Mr. and Mrs. Kirby, flanked by the twins, who were both wearing a look of importance. In the first row on the other side of the aisle sat Camilla Moss and her mother. I strained to see Camilla's face, and she seemed—if not as ecstatic as Kelly and her sister—not as miserable as I would have been in her shoes. She looked as if this was the most normal thing in the world. She sat up straight, made eye contact with other people, and even smiled. She appeared almost comfortable, and I thought how nice it must be to be that good an actress.

They called the meeting to order, but a whole boring hour went by, and then nearly another, before the clerk finally read from the sheet of paper he was holding:

"Whether Ernestine Kingston Moss, being a new resident of this county, should be entitled to

a zoning variance to institute a commercial enter-
prise on the site of her residence at 14 Slater
Drive, said residence being in Zone B of multiple
variance." He looked up at us. "Anyone wish to
speak on this matter?"

For a moment there was silence, then over on
our left a hand went up.

The clerk nodded and Theresa stood up, taking
a moment to rearrange her clothes, as if she
thought she was having her picture taken. Then she
cleared her throat.

"Well, Dave ... uh, your honor ..."

"Please state your name and address."

"Theresa Morgan, 117 Taylor Lane."

"You may proceed."

She looked a bit rattled for a moment, but after
clearing her throat, she began.

"I have lived in Old MacIntosh all my life, and
that is a good many years." Here she smiled coyly.
"More than I wish to admit to in this gathering."
There was a smattering of laughter and she went
on. "This is a very special small town and it has
laws about what we can do and what we can't do.
Now, some people coming from out of town may
find that strange, and think, 'It's just a law—and
laws are meant to be broken.' But I say, not here
they're not! Maybe in *big* places like Detroit or
Chicago or New York City, they wouldn't care a
whit who comes and goes and whether or not
they're into abiding by the law of the community.
In them places such a thing probably wouldn't
cause a ripple. But it would make many people

here nervous to have certain kinds of people around, plying their wares, *their foreign goods,* in our village. And I'm not ashamed to admit I'm one of them. I guess what I'm trying to say is that in Old MacIntosh, Vermont, we don't take to things that are un-American, and we don't like ripples. Thank you very much."

Theresa sat down with a self-satisfied smile on her face. It was obvious she thought the matter was all settled now, thanks to her. She had just performed a great service for the town and the Kirbys, among others, would love her for it.

And she *had* started the ball rolling. All around the room hands went up like Scud missiles as, one by one, people stood up and spoke in protest of Mrs. Moss starting her business. I still couldn't see Camilla's face, but I knew all too well what she was going through. Why had she come?

Then the chair recognized someone way in the front. When I heard "Camilla Moss, 14 Slater Drive," I bolted upright, straining to see.

She turned around to face the audience before she said anything more.

"I ... I just wanted to say that if you people are under the impression that my father is some kind of criminal, you couldn't be more wrong. He's a decent man who was just too trusting of some other men who really *were* crooks. And the unfair thing is, *they* didn't even have to go to jail!" Somebody must have pulled at her then, because she jerked to the side and looked down. "No! I'm *all right.*" Then she continued. "It's not fair not to let my mother own a business here just because of that. And the stuff she imports is really lovely. Anyway, if you say no, we'll just have to go somewhere else and then that town will be the lucky one because my mom is . . ." But here her voice started to break and she sat down abruptly.

There was an uncomfortable silence for a moment and I thought maybe it was all over. How could Camilla *do* that? I would have absolutely died. I would never even have come here in the first place.

Suddenly a movement next to me brought me up with a start. Before I could stop it, Paisley's arm was up, and so was Paisley.

"Paisley Gerard, 12 Ridge Road, owner of Paisley's Place," she began, and I froze as a slight titter rippled through the crowd. People turned in their seats as if a good show was going to start—one they'd seen before, one that had always given them a good laugh.

"I cannot believe what has gone on here tonight! *For shame! For shame!* I was born and brought up in this eden and I've lived here a good part of my life and while I know that some of our civic leaders are the most *narrow-minded, bigoted, pea-brained neanderthals* on the planet, I *did* think our Vermont soul had not flown off into the night." I tugged at her sleeve violently. You couldn't say things like that! She'd be arrested! But there was no stopping her. "I'm afraid you've really done it this time. You've *astonished* me. Yes, that's what you've done! You've *astonished* me. I must correct the observation made by my dear friend, Theresa Morgan. *If* the Mosses are forced to relocate, I hope they're not foolish enough to think they have to go all the way to Chicago or Detroit or even New York City to find people who will accept them. Vermont is a wonderful state. And there are many towns where I'm sure these good people would be given a hand up, and not pushed away."

She was flailing her arms and gesturing as she spoke, but I didn't look up and I tried not to hear, because I'd been through this before and I knew that the faces that had turned in our direction wore certain expressions: tolerant, amused. The way people look at a crazy person doing stunts in a sideshow. And I knew about the other people who hadn't turned around in their seats. I knew their faces too: stony, disapproving. "Making a spectacle of herself again," I'd heard one man say two years ago when she spoke up at a school board meeting over a sex education course for kindergarten. She was for that cause, too, but she lost. Just as she would probably lose this time. Paisley was always on one side, with the rest of the world—or at least the Old MacIntosh part of it—on the other.

So why did she bother? Sometimes I thought it was just to put me through this special kind of hell.

I stared straight ahead, counting the row of black buttons on the cardigan sweater that Jillie Barnes's mother had slung casually over her chair. Nine—or was it ten?—no, there were eleven if that was another button peeking out of the bottom where there was this nice cable stitch running around the edge. Mrs. Barnes was at the school a lot for meetings, and whenever I saw her, she always smiled and was real friendly. She was pretty too. With blonde hair that she wore pulled back with a little headband.

When Paisley finally sat down, like an exotic bag of laundry that someone had just tossed on the seat, Mr. Sinclair rose to agree with her and Mr. Reese from the pharmacy started to argue with him, and the clerk up in the front sounded the gavel and said it was getting late and they were going to have to table the Moss zoning ordinance until next week. So Paisley gathered up her skirts and announced that we were leaving. But as I started to get up, I noticed the Mosses heading for the door too.

"Let's wait a minute," I said.

"Why?"

"We don't want to bump into them," I said. But what could I have been thinking of? It was *exactly* what Paisley would want.

"Come on," she said, mumbling "Excuse me," as she pushed her way along the aisle, almost smothering people with her outfit as she brushed by them.

We reached the lobby just as Camilla and her mother were pushing open the glass doors and, although the rain had stopped, a cool blast of night air made me shiver.

"Wait!" Paisley called out, and Camilla's mother turned and stared at her, her eyes growing wide as my mother, her hair in disarray and wrapped in her blanket coat, hurled herself through the door ahead of the other people leaving the meeting. I hung back, trying to blend in with the crowd, and found myself next to Camilla.

"Oh," I said. "Hi."

"Hi," she said, smiling, like this was just an everyday occurrence and not one of the most embarrassing nights of her life.

We came out the door together, and I could see my mother huddled with hers at the entrance to the parking lot. I felt awkward, knowing I should say something, but feeling foolish if I said the truth: that I thought she was incredibly brave to speak up the way she did.

"You ... you were very good in there," I said.

"Naw, *I* wasn't. But your mom was! Thank her for me, okay?"

I looked at her, surprised. But of course she would think it was a kind gesture. She wouldn't know that Paisley had just adopted her family as her cause-of-the-week.

"Oh, don't worry, Paisley didn't do it for you."

"What do you mean?"

"I mean ... oh, nothing."

"Come on, tell me. Your mom was one of the few people on our side in there; you're telling me she *wasn't* on our side?"

"Oh, she was on your side all right. But it's just the way she is. I mean, she likes to be, what's the word—confrontational."

"It must be so great to have a mother like that. Well, gotta go. See you tomorrow!"

"Right. See you tomorrow."

Boy, they talk about the grass always being greener. But was Camilla off base or what? I went to the van and waited for Paisley to finish up whatever it was she was doing with Mrs. Moss.

It *had* gotten worse, I realized as my mother got in and started the van. And it wasn't just Linda's leaving. When I was little, it didn't matter so much, but now I was in junior high. I was almost a teenager and I had a *right* to be normal, to blend in, not to be the laughingstock of the whole town.

And feeling this way did not make me a bad person, I decided, as I turned and looked out the rain-spattered window, swallowing hard. No matter what stupid Camilla Moss said, it *didn't*.

Spirit Week was almost over and the last day, as always, was Sleepwalking Day. When I climbed onto the bus wearing my flannel nightgown and clutching my teddy bear I could tell even before I sat down that I was in trouble.

I'd been praying for a tornado—or any other natural disaster—to hit town before the flea market. But it didn't look like it was going to happen. The forecast said "brisk and sunny," so now my only hope of getting through it lay in gaining so much social standing from riding on the float in the morning (squeezed in, hopefully, next to Joey Whitelaw) that it would carry me through the rest of the day.

But the person with the keys to the float was staring at me now like I was her worst enemy.

"I love your jammies," I said right away, trying to get a laugh, trying to pretend that I didn't know from Kelly's prune face that she was annoyed.

"Thanks," she said acidly as she turned and stared out the window.

"Are you mad?" I asked.

94

"How could your mother have taken *their* side?"

"Listen, you're the one who wanted her to come to the meeting."

"I should have known better. My folks are *really annoyed*," she added, letting me know to what deep social depths I had tumbled.

"Well, it's not *my* fault," I said. "I don't know why you're mad at me."

"Can't you *control* her?" she asked, like my mom was a dog that was digging up the Kirby garden.

"No," I said quietly. "As a matter of fact, I can't."

She sighed deeply. "I guess you can't," she said. Luckily for me, if there was one thing a Kirby liked to do, it was forgive. But then she seemed to have second thoughts; maybe I shouldn't be let off so easily. "But what about next week's meeting? Can you at least promise she won't be there and do it again?"

I swallowed hard. "Sure," I said, nodding.

"By the way, I saw you talking to Camilla Moss afterward. You're not getting to be *friends* with her, are you?"

"Of course not!" I said.

"Well, that's a relief," she said.

I could tell by her expression that peace had been restored, so for the rest of the bus ride we could concentrate on watching the kids as they came on board in their nightgowns and pajamas. When I saw Camilla in a flannel nightgown almost identical to mine, I pretended to be picking lint off Billy Boy's fur so I wouldn't have to say hi. Hi's and hello's on the bus are sort of a big deal in our school. I don't get many, that's why I'm grateful to have a reserved seat next to Kelly so at least I'm not alone if I'm snubbed. Some days Jillie Barnes seems to include us in her smile, some days she doesn't. That's just the way it is. Today when she came on, all the boys started to hoot and whistle because she was wearing a burgundy-lace robe from Victoria's Secret. I could see that she had a T-shirt and shorts on underneath, so I'm sure they could, too, but that's just the way boys act around Jillie. Most of the girls didn't even try to compete. Certainly not me. Why do you think I brought the teddy bear? Just in case the flannel nightgown didn't get the message across that what we're dealing with here is a nine-year-old, I figured Billy Boy would do the trick.

As we hurried off the bus in front of the school, I deliberately didn't look in Camilla's direction. Some other day I'd be extra friendly and make it up to her, I promised myself. But there was too much at stake tomorrow to make a wrong move today.

The next morning as I hurried up the Kirbys' driveway I could see Phil, the Kirbys' handyman, standing next to one of their trucks with a cup of coffee in his hand. He was a big, burly man with little tufts of gray hair sticking out from under his cap. Gina, Jillie, and Bobby had gotten there ahead of me.

"Hi, Phil!" I said.

"Hiya, sweetheart. Look, I gave the truck a real good cleanup for you kids. There was lots of wood chips and some sawdust in the back. But now—clean as a whistle!"

He was standing back with such pride on his face that I knew a look of astonishment was called for and I tried to work one up, but it was early in the morning and I don't think it was happening.

"Gee, that's really nice," Jillie said.

"Beautiful," I added lamely.

The side door banged shut as Kelly came running toward us.

"I just called Maddy's house and there's no answer, so they must be on their way over."

That number sure was getting around.

"What stuff does she have?" Jillie asked.

"She has the balloons, but I have the panther inside."

"Who has the streamers?"

"I have," Gina answered, holding up a six-pack of pink Charmin.

"Is that stuff going to work?" Jillie asked, sounding annoyed. "Why didn't you get regular streamers?"

"The crepe paper stuff wasn't the right shade of pink, so I decided to go with this," she said, pouting to show that she resented the question. "*I* think it'll work great."

"I hope so," Jillie mumbled. "Come on, we don't have much time. We'd better start with that."

"Why don't we wait till Joey gets here," Bobby whined.

"Oh you know he's probably with Maddy and they're always late. Let's just do it!" Jillie said.

So we started winding toilet paper around the truck. Only it was a windy October morning and you know how toilet paper is made with little squares so it'll tear easily? In a few moments the Kirbys' driveway had all these little pink squares wafting in the breeze. Every time we thought the "streamers" were secure, the wind would gust and tear a few more off.

No matter how many times we circled the truck in a vain attempt to give it a festive air, by the time Gina and Kelly came out of the house with the centerpiece of the float, the place looked like there'd been a terrorist attack in a public rest room. Pink toilet paper squares were everywhere: in the bushes, hanging from the limbs of trees, even on the signpost that proudly displayed a duck with the name *Kirby* carved in its feathers. If there'd been some shaving cream on the mailbox it would have looked like a Halloween hit.

The panther didn't look too great either. He was actually an old stuffed lion, so we had cut off his mane and rubbed his golden face with black Magic Marker and put him in pink. And nobody had remembered to get a box to sit him on, so he wasn't as big as we'd hoped he'd be. But the pink tutu *was* cute (even if you couldn't really see it without climbing inside the truck), which offset the fact that the pink rollers kept slipping out of the black wig.

"Oh, God," Kelly said, "the rollers are never going to stay!"

"How about safety pins?" somebody said.

"Scotch tape?"

Phil reached over and examined the wig.

"Rubber bands," he pronounced. "I got some in the glove compartment."

"You're a lifesaver!"

"This is a very cute idea," Phil said as he stood by, waiting to drive the float over for us when we had finished working on it. "Which one of you guys thought it up?"

"Who was it?" Jillie said. "It was you, Gina, wasn't it?"

"Nope, it wasn't me."

"I don't remember," Bobby said. "Who did think of it?"

"I know," Gina said. "It was Camilla Moss. Remember, she came to that first meeting."

"That's right," Bobby said. "That's before we knew who she was. She's not riding with us, is she?"

"Of course not," Kelly said. "What made you think that?"

"Because it *was* her idea. Isn't that the rule?"

"No, it is *not* the rule," Kelly snapped. "Not when it's *my* truck."

"I tell you, that's a sad situation," Phil intervened. "But I hear they're letting him out early, so it'll be over pretty soon and they can get on with their lives."

"As long as they don't get on with them around here," Gina said, and she and Kelly giggled.

"Ah, that's not right. They should let that

woman open her store. What are they gonna do, move somewhere else?"

"Why not? I mean, why did they pick our town in the first place?" Kelly asked.

Phil looked over and nodded at me as if he'd just remembered who I was.

"Your mom did good the other night, Holly. I was there."

I could feel myself flush, but I was saved from answering him because just then Kelly looked over my shoulder and said, "Finally!" I turned around as a red sports car pulled into the driveway and Maddy Brown hopped out gracefully, followed by Joey Whitelaw clutching a handful of pink helium balloons.

"Sorr-ee. It took us forever to get these blown up," she said.

I tried to get a look at Maddy's mother, but the sun was shining on the windshield so all I could see was a blur of a face with dark glasses and lots of blonde hair piled high on her head.

When she backed out of the driveway without a word, I turned my attention back to the dynamic duo. I've decided I don't like Joey Whitelaw after all. Not one bit. He's just too tall.

"Are you almost finished?" Maddy asked hopefully.

"Not *quite*," Jillie said.

"That little girl was very good too," Phil went on, still talking about the meeting as if he hadn't even noticed the others arriving.

"You mean Camilla Moss?" Kelly said, making a face.

"Hey, yeah," Joey said. "I heard about that. She's got guts, you know?"

"Look who's got a crush on Big Bird!" Maddy said, rolling her eyes and laughing, even though it was pretty obvious she was really annoyed. Joey gave her a look, but she pretended not to notice. She'd been resting against a rock while she watched them struggling to fasten the helium balloons to the truck. "You know, I hate to say it, but those streamers look pretty lame!"

Jillie shot Gina a look. "I *told* you we should have used regular streamers!"

"But they were the wrong color—"

"Careful, you guys!" Maddy warned as Bobby almost let one of the balloons escape. "You have to be so careful with those things. We used them on the set one time, and they deflated too soon and they looked just awful by the time we were shooting the party scene."

"*What* party scene?" Jillie said, beginning to sound a bit testy.

"The party scene we were *filming*," Maddy said in the tone of voice she used sometimes as if she were making her acceptance speech at the Academy Awards. It usually shut people up.

"A scene in a *movie?*" Bobby asked.

"Uh, actually, that time it was a commercial. For Dr. Pepper."

"You were in a commercial for *Dr. Pepper?*" Bobby repeated, sounding so awed that Jillie snapped around and I thought for a minute she was going to do something spontaneous and unrehearsed with the hammer she was holding.

"Of course I was, but let's not talk about it, *please*. I know how boring shoptalk can be if you're not in the business!"

I finished twisting the last bit of wig into a pink roller, secured it with a rubber band, and then stood back to admire my handiwork.

"I think we're all set," Jillie said finally, still glowering at Bobby.

Joey looked at the panther and then at me. "You did *good*," he said, giving me a little Gumby smile.

Too tall . . . too tall . . .

We were all strangely silent driving over to the school, which may have been a premonition, but I think we were just afraid that any laughter or sudden movement would cause more toilet paper to rip or a roller to fall off (my particular dread), or a helium balloon to ascend prematurely into the heavens.

But we needn't have worried. The seniors had constructed an atomic laboratory on a Ford pickup truck, with orange and blue bubbles coming out of a huge test tube and a neon sign that read: NUKE THE PANTHERS.

And the toilet paper kept on doing its thing the whole morning: Here a square, there a square. We lost two of the balloons before the game even started, and we had to lift the panther up for him to be seen. So, of course, we didn't win.

That's the bad news.

And the good news?

My fantasy came true. Maybe it happened by accident, or maybe somebody planned it, but when we climbed on board to hoot and shout at halftime, Maddy rode on one side between Jillie and Bobby (which could have gotten ugly) and Joey Whitelaw rode—you guessed it—squeezed in next to me.

Oh, and he was right—I *did* do a good job. Throughout the whole parade—even when we hoisted the panther up in the air—the rollers stayed on. Unfortunately, the wig fell off.

When I finally found my mother's booth at the flea market, I could tell that she was having a really good time. She was sitting on a high red stool, her skirts hiked up over her knees, her bare legs poking out like sticks that ended in rough leather boots. She was munching on an apple and she looked so contented I knew she must have sold some things.

"Hi, honeybabes! Just in time. Where are your friends?"

"They're at the pizza booth. I just came by to say 'hi.' Did you sell much?"

"Yeah, I did. And it's supposed to get busier now that the game is over! So, did your float win?"

"Uh, no, we didn't."

"Too bad, but you don't look too disappointed. Listen, I need some change and some coffee. Can you hold the fort?"

"Oh, gee, I can't, Mom. I gotta run."

"Please? Just for five minutes? You can play store, like you used to when you were little. You can even dress up like you used to, if you want."

She took a beaded hat with a long ostrich feather and stuck it on my head.

"Stop it!"

"Wow. Sorry."

"That's okay," I said, smoothing my hair down with my hand.

"Listen, I promise I'll be back in ten minutes and if I see any of your friends, I'll tell them where you are!" she said, and she disappeared into the crowd before I could stop her. Terrific.

Leaning against the stool, I looked around and saw that most of what she'd brought were old dresses—what she called "vintage clothing"—along with tiny bits of jewelry made with jet stones and something called marcasite that looked like tiny little diamonds. I have to admit that sometimes I think the jewelry is kind of neat. There were mostly pins and some earrings; it was the kind of jewelry they used to wear long ago in a time they called the "Roaring Twenties." Some of the little evening bags were pretty too. Most of them were covered with sequins, and as I looked them over now I remembered how much fun I used to have when I was little and played dress up. I felt lucky then to have Paisley for a mother. Linda used to come over with a girl we knew in kindergarten named Arlene, and we'd put on the old clothes and the jewelry and carry the sequined bags. It was like having this wonderful attic to rummage around in, only the attic was our whole house. But Arlene moved away in first grade, and pretty soon it was only at Halloween that I felt lucky, and then I stopped feeling lucky at all. Now all I got was this stiff, cramped feeling. And on top of it all, making things worse, was the feeling of shame for *being* ashamed.

But at least there were no pieces of broken-down furniture—just some prints, sketches of flowers and birds that Paisley calls "botanicals." And last but not least, of course, there were the paisley shawls, dozens of them draped over every spare inch of the ten-by-eight-foot space that I had wanted to avoid today more than any other place on the planet.

"Holly?" I looked up and saw Camilla Moss standing in front of me, holding one of Paisley's shawls.

I had seen her at the game sitting over to the side with Nancy, but I'd hardly spoken to her since the meeting the other night. Now, without even thinking about what I was doing, I reached over and snatched the shawl out of her hands.

"Don't touch that!" I said.

Her mouth dropped open. "What is your problem? Do you *mind?* I'm buying one of these. I was just trying to pick which one."

"Oh," I said, letting the shawl go limp and, after a second's pause, handing it back to her. But I stood there, still wary, waiting to call her bluff when she snuck away. I would yell after her then, "Phony baloney!" and let her know that *I* knew she wasn't really buying one.

"What do you think?" she said, holding up another shawl, this time a black one with green and dark red paisley swirls. There were roses mixed into the design, and it was one of the prettiest.

I nodded. "It's pretty, I guess."

"You don't like it? Be honest. Really, I'd like your opinion. You like the green better?" she said, lifting one that was pale green with rust and gold.

I felt uncomfortable because she was pretending this was a perfectly normal conversation, like we were friends or something.

"I don't *know*," I said testily.

"But you live with this stuff, you must know something!"

Just then Paisley reappeared, tucking a roll of dollar bills into a hidden pocket of her long skirt as she slipped quickly back behind the table.

"Hi there," she said to Camilla, smiling. "I'm Paisley Gerard, Holly's mother."

"Hi. I'm ... Camilla Moss?" she said, with a small, confused smile.

"Oh, of course," Paisley said, looking embarrassed as she rolled her eyes. "Don't mind me." And she laughed, and then Camilla laughed too, giggling as if they were friends sharing a secret.

"I'm trying to decide which shawl to buy. They're all so pretty."

"That one you've got in your hand is one of my favorites. See the roses? That makes it special. You don't get that very often."

"Yeah, I think you're right. I'm gonna take it."

"Great," Paisley said, and she pulled a bag out from under the card table and began to fold the shawl.

Now Camilla had moved to the used clothes. "Oh, wow," she said. "Vintage clothing!"

"You like?"

"I *love!*"

"Not many kids appreciate the workmanship on some of these things." Paisley went over and pulled out a pea green crepe dress from the twenties. "Now, grant you the color's not my favorite, but feel. It's crepe de chine." The dress had a big stain on the front, but Paisley grabbed the shawl with the green and gold swirls and, shaking it out, draped it across the front. "Voilà! Good as new!"

"Hey, this stuff is *neat,*" Gina said, as she arrived with some of the other kids and crowded in behind Camilla.

"Look at this, isn't it *neat?*" she said again, holding out the pea green dress with the stain just as Maddy joined them. It was my worst nightmare, and it was going to get worse.

Maddy leaned across the table and laid her hand on Gina's arm. "It's dirty," she mouthed and then quickly dropped her eyes, pretending to look at the jewelry.

It had happened. I was caught. But she just continued to browse through the jewelry, ignoring me and not touching anything, as if she was afraid she might soil her hands. Finally she looked up and our eyes met.

"Why didn't you tell me you were working here?"

I swallowed hard. "I'm not ... really."

"Hey, watch it kids. Don't mess things up."

How could they mess things up?

"Oh, sorry, Mrs. Gerard," Kelly said, quickly putting back a black lace flapper outfit. "It's just that they're so—"

"Funky!" Jillie said. "Wouldn't it be neat to go to the Halloween dance in one of these?" she added.

"Yeah, sure, but look at the price tag," Gina said.

I was trying to pretend I wasn't there, you know? Sort of like "Beam me up, Scotty" in "Star Trek." But I wasn't entirely successful because I couldn't help noticing that Camilla and my mother had moved over to the corner and were having a quiet conversation.

I shouldn't be surprised that Paisley and Camilla Moss got along. Both enjoyed being weirdos. Both didn't mind being talked about, being laughed at. I could feel a kind of rage building up inside me, but I couldn't really justify it. I mean, Paisley wasn't doing anything particularly bizarre. And the kids seemed to really be enjoying going through the clothes and the jewelry. All except Maddy of course, who stood apart, still glaring at me. When I couldn't stand it another minute, I slipped around the table and went over to her.

"What's the matter, why do you keep staring at me?"

"I thought you said your mother was an antiques dealer," she said, in a low voice, her eyes slicing into me like swords.

I swallowed hard. "She *is*," I said defiantly.

109

She nodded. "Oh, right." From somewhere out in space I could hear people laughing as Maddy shook her head in bewilderment. "I thought you meant *real* antiques. It's one thing to be embarrassed, Holly. I understand that, I really do." Here she put her hand on my shoulder, as if she were comforting me at a funeral. "I can even feel *sorry* for you. But dishonesty is something else. You *lied* to me, Holly Gerard. And friends don't lie to one another." Then she said, "See you guys later!" and turned on her heel and flounced down the dirt path, through a jumble of handmade patchwork pot holders and hand-carved decoys, past used furniture and old photographs, and disappeared into the crowd.

I stood there frozen for a moment, sure that I would never ever be able to move from the spot and go on pretending that I was just another kid in town. Maddy Brown in one minute had stripped my bones, left me exposed for exactly what I was. Why had I tried to pretend? Because I didn't want what had just happened to happen, that's why. But she was right, I had lied, and the friendship was over and it was all my fault.

"You should have told her off."

I whirled around to see Camilla standing right behind me. "It's none of your business," I said hotly. "You don't know anything about it."

"Oh no? How much do I have to know? That little snot insulted your mother, *that's* the bottom line. What's the matter with you, don't you have any loyalty?"

She was looking at me as if she couldn't believe what she'd just seen.

"Let's go get a Coke," somebody said.

My mother looked over at Camilla. "Remember what I said!"

Camilla smiled at Paisley. "I will. And thanks!"

"You coming?" she asked.

I shook my head. I just wanted to crawl under the table and die. I didn't have the energy to join the others and pretend anymore.

She shrugged her shoulders and hurried to catch up with Jillie and Gina and the others, not seeming to realize she hadn't been invited. Her gall just added to my bad mood.

"Wait up, you guys! I've got *news!*" she called after them.

And would you believe it? They turned around and waited.

"*What about* this one?" Camilla said, holding a silver shift up against her as she twirled in front of the mirror. I hesitated, trying to share her enthusiasm, attempting desperately to see this as fun and the dress as a costume. But the dust kept getting in the way. Why couldn't I feel like I did in kindergarten: so lucky to have all these things to choose from? "Well?" she repeated.

"It's nice," I said, shrugging my shoulders.

"Are you sure your mother really meant I could borrow any of these for the dance?" she said, holding a lace number out now.

"Look, you're the one she promised. If that's what she said, that's what she meant."

I couldn't have been more surprised when Camilla told me about the deal she'd struck with my mother. The girl sure had nerve! But if Paisley wanted to lend her a dress for the dance, so what? I figured it wasn't going to change my life any.

"But some of this stuff is gorgeous. What if I spill on it or tear it or something?"

"Trust me, Paisley never sells any of these, and

what she sells goes 'as is.' You can't do anything that hasn't been done already."

"You know which one I really love?" she asked, her eyes shining.

"Which one?"

"That one," she said, poking her finger at a ruby-sequined number. I knew it well. It had been one of my favorites too.

"Take it," I said, enjoying the fact that I could be generous with stuff that wasn't mine.

"You really think so?"

"Sure."

"You are so lucky."

"Oh, yeah."

"What are *you* going to wear?"

"What do you mean?"

"To the Halloween dance. Are you going as a flapper too?"

"Oh, *no.*"

"Why not? The rest of us are."

"What do you mean, 'the rest of us'?"

"Jillie, Maddy, Kelly, Gina ..."

"Where are you getting the dresses?" *And when did you get so chummy with them?*

"I thought you knew. Your mom said anyone who wanted could borrow them for the dance."

"I didn't know that—I thought it was just you!"

"Well at first, yeah. That's what she told me at the flea market. But when I told the others about it, they all wanted in. So I checked with your mom and she said fine. She said they weren't selling anyway."

"Oh, I didn't know."

"So what are you going to go as?"

"I don't think I'll even go."

"Because Maddy Brown hurt your feelings?"

"That's a stupid, rotten thing to say! You don't know anything about it!"

"I know that you're still bummed about it, right?"

I shrugged my shoulders.

"I don't understand it," she said. "I've gotta be honest with you, I just don't understand it."

"Understand what?"

"Why you'd want to be friends with *her*."

"Come on. She's one of the most popular kids around here."

"But she's such a phony. And if she doesn't like you—"

"But she did! At least she did until she found out about Paisley."

"See, that's what I mean! I just don't get it. Why would you want to be friends with someone who dumps on your mother? Who doesn't like the *real you*."

"The real me—yeah, right, the tinker's daughter."

"The what?"

"Never mind."

"No, tell me. What'd you call yourself?"

I heard myself sigh. "The tinker's daughter," I said.

"What's a *tinker*?"

I took a deep breath, wrapping my arms tighter around my knees as I sat on the floor watching her still picking through the clothes.

"Tinkers are kind of like gypsies. They travel

around Europe in wagons with bells on them so people will know they're coming. They mainly fix things, I think."

"So what does that have to do with *you?*"

I smiled. One part of me was wondering why I was telling this to someone I hardly knew, while the rest of me was thinking how good it felt to be able to talk about it.

"When I was little, Paisley told me about the tinkers. She had heard about them from her grandmother and she said that she would have loved to have been one. For a long time after that, I was afraid she'd come home in some kind of wagon and want us to start living like gypsies. Then I got to worrying that she'd just settle for hanging bells on the van."

"I hope you don't mind me saying this—I mean, we're not good friends or anything—but you seem awfully hung up on your mother. What about your dad? What's he like?"

I stared at her, and then I swallowed hard before I spoke. "I don't know."

"You never met him?"

I shook my head. "Nope."

She hesitated a moment and I figured I'd finally shut up Miss Know-It-All, but obviously she was just thinking, because she began to nod her head and then she said, "You know, that's really *great.*"

"What?"

"It's great! Don't you see that? You've got *two* parents, right, same as everybody else on the planet?"

"Yeah?"

"So how do you know that your old man wasn't some real dignified old fuddy-duddy. And you're a mixture of both of them, so you came out nice and normal!"

I thought about it for a minute. "I don't see Paisley with an old fuddy-duddy. I always figured he was some kind of loony. Especially since she wouldn't tell me anything about him."

"But that's just it! Don't you see? She was probably ashamed because he was so dull and colorless. I mean, if he was the lead guitarist with the Grateful Dead, you don't think she would've bragged about it?" She must have seen the grin spreading over my face because she went on, "I mean, if you're going to grow up without a father, you've gotta make it work for you. Don't you know that yet? You gotta make things work for you!"

"Thank you, Camilla. I know you're trying to make me feel better. And you have, even though I know I'm still stuck."

"Who says you're stuck?" All the time we were talking she kept going through the dresses. I kept thinking she had made a choice, but then she'd change her mind and put it back and pick another one. "Nobody's stuck if they don't wanna be."

"Camilla, come off it. You can't change who you are."

"Well, not now, maybe. But you can change who you're gonna be!"

"What are you talking about?"

"I mean, we're still kids. Who are you going to be when you grow up?"

116

"A grown-up version of *me*, stupid. Who did you think?"

"Oh." She frowned then, as if I was saying something really strange, instead of something dead-on obvious.

"Who are *you* going to be, Miss Moss?" I asked, hoping sufficient sarcasm was dripping from my voice.

She shrugged her shoulders then and her eyes opened wide. "I dunno," she said. "I'm not there yet. But I know one thing!" And she smiled this real pleased-with-herself smile.

"Yeah?"

"I'll be someone *who's never been before!*"

"What?"

"Sure. And so will you!"

"I don't get it. Where'd you come up with *that?*"

"From my grandmother. That's what she used to say when she saw a newborn baby. She'd say, 'This here is so-and-so, someone who's never been before.' I always liked it and I think about it once in a while. When I grow up and I'm away from all this, that's who I'll be: kind of like a blank slate and a fresh start—you know what I'm saying?" I nodded, because suddenly I did know. "You can use it if you want. Maybe it'll make *you* feel better too." I didn't say anything and there was silence for a second. Then she shifted the subject.

"But listen, about Maddy Brown. If I were you I'd cut her dead in the halls. I wouldn't even speak to her when you're at your locker."

"You really think so?" I said, remembering how

she'd ignored me when we reached the locker at the same time this morning, and how she'd sat with Jillie's crowd at lunch.

"Definitely. That's what *I'd* do."

The door slammed in the shop and Paisley's voice rang through to the back room, where we were sitting.

"Is that Camilla I hear in there with you, Holly? Let me see what she picked!"

Camilla took the ruby dress and walked through to the front to show it to Paisley.

"Hey, nice choice! You've got a good eye, doesn't she, Holly?"

I nodded.

"Thank you so much! I told the others and they'll be stopping by."

"Only because you were the one who asked, Camilla. I think it's a neat idea! I'd love to be there and see some of these old things in action again— fun!"

Camilla wrapped the dress in tissue and was folding it carefully into a plastic bag she'd brought over when she suddenly stopped.

"Wait a minute—I have a great idea!"

A flash of terror—call it a premonition—seared through me.

"What kind of a great idea?" I asked. But when she answered, she was talking to Paisley.

"We need a third chaperone. Mr. Walters backed out, and I was going to ask Ms. Crimmins, the gym teacher, but she's no fun. And they said we could ask one of the parents—"

"Camilla," I said, trying to interrupt. But I was too late.

"So, would you like to be one of our chaperones at the dance, Mrs. Gerard?"

"Hey, call me Paisley. What a neat idea! I'm really flattered that you'd ask me. I'd *love* to be a chaperone. Especially for something funky like this."

I stood there, stunned, while Camilla thanked my mother a few dozen times and Paisley thanked Camilla a few dozen times.

Finally Camilla left.

"Mom, you can't do this," I said, noticing how shaky my voice sounded.

"Why not?"

"Because you always made fun of the mothers who did this sort of thing, like Mrs. Kirby and Linda's mom!"

"Well gee, can't you at least appreciate the irony of *me* being a chaperone? Can you imagine anything I'd censor? You kids should have a blast!"

"See, that's what I mean! You're only doing it to ... to ridicule everything. You know that. Please don't do that to me," I said, my voice wearing thin and giving out before I'd had a chance to put up much of a struggle.

"I suppose it would never occur to you that she might actually think I would make a good chaperone?" I wasn't sure but I thought there was a little catch in her voice. "Especially at a Halloween dance," she added.

Was that it? Was Camilla making fun of Paisley?

Here was a mom who could show up "as is" and get the weirdest-costume award.

It was such a sneaky thing for her to do! And just when I was beginning to think we might have something in common. She never mentioned it the whole time we were talking in the back room and she must have been planning it all along. It was like the flapper dresses they were all borrowing.

Suddenly the situation was getting out of hand. I had always tried to keep everything in my life in a separate place, like eggs in a carton: school, home, mother, friends. But Camilla Moss was messing things up.

The telephone rang just then, and I ran into the parlor and grabbed the phone.

"Hello?" I barked.

"Hello, Holly?" The voice on the other end, with its faintly southern lilt, fairly chirped with friendliness.

She had never called me before and now just when I thought it was all over, here she was. I stood there for a moment, too surprised to speak.

"Maddy?" I managed to reply.

I don't know whether Maddy's mother always drove like that, but when the red convertible came tearing down the school's long, winding driveway it was going so fast I didn't think it was going to stop in time. But it did, and swooping us up like we were just parcels standing on the sidewalk, Fleur Brown took off again up the hill without saying a word.

Neither of them spoke. No "Hi, Mom," no "Hi, Maddy." And Maddy and I didn't speak either. She seemed to be very interested in the scenery outside her window, as if she were a stranger who'd never come this way before. So I took the opportunity to study Maddy's mother. The brief glimpse I'd had of her the day in the Kirbys' driveway was only a hint of the woman sitting in the driver's seat.

She had golden hair piled up so high on her head that it made me suspect right away that it wasn't all hers. I was pretty sure that part of it—the top part—was some kind of wig. And I figured that her incredibly long red nails weren't real either. She was smoking, tapping her cigarette out in the little ashtray in the middle, and the smoke was beginning to bother me, but I wasn't sure if it would be rude to open the window and we were almost there, so I decided to suffer in silence.

Maddy had taken me by surprise when she'd called yesterday. Her father was coming up unexpectedly this afternoon, she'd gushed. And she was really dying to have me meet him. Would I be able to come over after school if her mother picked us up?

I was thrilled, of course—confused and surprised and thrilled. Maybe it wasn't over after all.

Seven minutes after we'd left the school grounds we drove through the pillars that said STONEGATE, then up one of the side streets to the right, and into one of the driveways. Mrs. Brown turned the engine off, jumped out of the car, and hurried inside without even turning to look at Maddy and me. It sure was strange. I mean, here I was, a guest in their house for the very first time, and she was totally ignoring me. Of course, she was totally ignoring her daughter, too, so I was in good company.

Only when her mother was out of sight did Maddy turn and speak to me.

"You'll have to forgive Fleur. This arrangement makes her crazy enough, but she's really nervous about Daddy dropping by."

We were walking up to the side entrance of the condo.

"What arrangement?" I asked.

"My being up *here*. Going to school here," she said, in a tone of voice that made it clear she thought it was a really stupid question. As if I should *know* what arrangement.

"You don't really want to be here, do you?"

She looked at me strangely for a second, and then she just said, "Sure I do." But I don't think that's what she had started to say.

We came into the kitchen and Maddy's mother was standing at the counter looking out the window. Everything was spotless, as if it were a picture in a magazine. I thought of our kitchen at home and I almost gagged.

"Mom, this is Holly Gerard, a *friend* of mine," Maddy said pointedly.

Mrs. Brown turned from the window and gave me a big smile framed in bright red lipstick. Then she blinked her eyes rapidly, with what I was pretty sure were false eyelashes. It was as if she were meeting me for the first time, as if her driving me over here somehow didn't count.

"Hello there, Holly! It's always so nice to meet one of Maddy's friends!"

"Hi there, Mrs. Brown," I said in my best voice, the one I reserve for people like the principal and parents I don't know very well.

"Don't call me Mrs. Brown," she said. "It's Ms. Caldwell."

"Mom, is there any food in this place?" Maddy asked, interrupting.

"I don't know. Check the fridge."

Maddy went over and opened the refrigerator door. "Didn't Ruthanne go to the store?" she asked, in a voice my mom would have called *bratty*.

"I told her to."

"But did she go?"

123

"Why don't you ask her? I don't think she's left yet."

Maddy turned to me. "I'll be right back," she said and stormed out of the kitchen, leaving me standing there feeling like a broom, all stiff and awkward and ugly next to Maddy's mom, who wore more makeup than I've ever seen anyone's mother wear. Especially in a kitchen.

Maddy was back in a flash and went over and opened a cupboard above the stove.

"Here, we have some crackers," she said, tossing them on the table. "But *no* cheese, *no* fruit. I say we get rid of her. Honest and truly, there has to be somebody better, even around here."

I winced when she said that and I hoped nobody noticed. And they didn't, because Maddy and her mom were locked in an intense dialogue that seemed very private, as if it were some kind of shorthand that only they could understand.

"She's the best. Honest, baby."

"That's hard to believe. She moves my stuff! Haven't you told her not to move my stuff?"

"I have. I think she's just trying to do a good job."

"Well, tell her to keep her hands off my stuff or it's *good-bye*. You want me to tell her?"

Her mother shrugged. "You want to tell her, you tell her. Maybe she'll listen to you. But I gave her a list this morning," she said, gesturing to the crackers. "I know I wrote down *fruit*. What can I tell you?"

Just then a horn sounded outside and Mrs.

Brown—Ms. Caldwell—turned and looked out the window.

"Oh, God, he's here. You kids beat it."

"Mom! *I* want to see him too."

"Later. Let me handle it for now."

"Look, it's not your career on the line—"

"Let me *start*. Just remember—"

"I know, I know," she mumbled under her breath, *"Vermont eyes."*

Maddy's mother nodded as she went out the side door, and a minute later we could hear her raspy, high-pitched voice greeting Maddy's father.

Maddy got two cans of Coke out of the refrigerator and handed me one as I followed her down an immaculate white hallway into a bedroom on the left.

Her room was small and pretty, with pink flowers all over the bedspread and the curtains and a small chair. A bookcase took up a whole wall, and it was loaded with every kind of stuffed animal you could imagine.

"Gee, you have a pretty room."

"It's okay."

She went over to a small TV in the corner and switched it on to "General Hospital," then opened her Coke and sprawled on the bed. We watched in silence for a while, with her on the bed and me sitting stiffly on the chair, and when the show was over, we had finished all the crackers and I was still starved and she still had a nervous look on her face.

Finally I said, "What's going on?"

125

She looked over at me as if she hadn't heard me. "What?"

"You invited me here to meet your father, but I mean, you're not even meeting him."

"Didn't you want to come? Is this some kind of big problem or something?"

I swallowed hard. I think I had always known down deep inside that Maddy was spoiled, conceited, and, let's face it, not the nicest kid you'd ever meet. But up to now I was willing to make excuses for her—to Camilla and, most of all, to myself. But the way Maddy was acting now was just so plain ugly I had to admit it: I was finally meeting the real Maddy Brown. I was so sorry I had come, but what could I do about it now?

"You seem upset about something, that's all," I finally said.

"Oh, no, everything's just *fine.*"

"Oprah" came on then, and we watched for a while in silence. It was all about mothers who stole their teenage daughters' boyfriends. We're talking fifteen- and sixteen-year-old boys, and they were going out with somebody's mother! But it turns out the mothers never had much fun in high school, like they were fat or something, and they were just trying to make up for it. I thought about Paisley, and I knew for certain that here at least was something she'd never pull. Then I thought of Maddy's mom and I wasn't so sure.

"Wait here," Maddy said suddenly, and she jumped off the bed and flew out of the room like she was going to explode.

126

I could hear her calling, "Mom? Dad-dy?" and then the muffled sound of them answering from the living room. Then I think all of them must have gone off somewhere to talk, and I was left sitting all alone in the room like Miss Stupid. After a few minutes, I turned off the television and walked over to the window. You couldn't see too much except other condos, and I thought how much prettier my view was. Our place certainly wasn't as nice as this, but outside the view was a whole lot better because it was just trees and woods, and at night, a whole lot of sky filled with stars. I craned my neck but could see only a teeny bit of sky between the two condos across the way. I wouldn't like living here one bit.

I could hear voices being raised, and the feeling that I was an intruder grew on me with each passing minute. Whatever was going on, I didn't want any part of it. There was a bus down the hill that ran on the half hour and would take me into town. And from there I could walk home. I glanced at my watch; it was twenty after four—I'd have to hurry.

I decided to just walk straight back to the kitchen, pick up my book bag, and head out the door. If they saw me, I'd just say I'd remembered that I had a term paper to do and had to go to the library.

I slipped out the door quietly, but I had only gone a few feet down the hall when a man's voice made me freeze.

"Now you're absolutely sure you're involved in school activities?"

"I told you, Harvey. She just rode on the float in the goddamned football parade."

"They took pictures and they'll probably be in the school newspaper. I'll send you one," Maddy added. "So will you tell Uncle Pete to set me up for some auditions? They're going to forget I exist!"

"Not so fast, young lady. Now, you've got this nice little friend—what's her name?"

"Holly Gerard."

Something in the way Maddy said my name made my stomach do a flip-flop.

"I don't know why acting like a normal girl should be so hard on you, Madison," her father said.

"*Most* fathers wouldn't have made it part of the divorce agreement!" Fleur said.

"Well, you didn't want a custody battle, Fleur."

"No, but you didn't have to bury us up in this hellhole."

"Now, now, it can't be that bad. It's a bit in the backwoods, but it is very scenic. But tell me more about this friend of yours. You're sure she's not one of the flashy ones, you know, twelve going on thirty?"

Maddy gave a hoot. "Dad, *trust* me, she's totally out of it." Then her voice changed, as if she knew she'd said the wrong thing. "I mean," she corrected herself, "I picked her because I know you were right and I needed to take some time out and get grounded. Believe me, you will love her. We get along just *great* and she's become a real role model for me, just like you wanted." Maddy let out a huge sigh. "And just like you predicted, Daddy, thanks to her I'm starting to see the world through *Vermont eyes.*"

"Well, that's good to hear, Madison. You say she's here right now?"

"Yeah, she's in my room. You want to meet her?"

"I'd love to."

I tried to get out the door before Maddy saw me, but I wasn't fast enough.

"Where are you going?" she demanded.

"Oh, uh ... I just realized I have a paper due. I'm just gonna grab the bus."

"But you haven't met my dad. That's what you're here for, you know!"

She said it as if it were a job I was being paid to do. But I was so confused I just stumbled after her, and as I entered the room a burly man with a mustache stood up from where he had been sitting across from Maddy's mother and held out his hand.

"So this is Madison's new friend. Your name is ..."

"Holly," I answered in a low voice. "Holly Gerard."

"Pretty name. I can't tell you how pleased I am to make your acquaintance. Why don't you sit down."

"I'm sorry, sir, but I have to get to the library."

"Oh. Well, looks like we have a serious student here. But that's okay with me. Maybe we'll meet again. Why don't you see your little friend out, Madison."

Maddy smiled sweetly. "Sure, Dad."

As we went out the front door I glanced at my

watch and realized that now I'd have to wait for the five o'clock bus. But Maddy made no move to walk me to the bus stop, of course. Instead, she turned to go back inside as if I were being dismissed.

"Maddy, can I ask you something?"

"Sure," she said, turning and giving me that wide-eyed look that was now so familiar.

"What was the name of the movie you were in with Kevin Costner?"

"What? I never made a movie with Kevin Costner."

"I didn't think so. Did you ever make any movie? With anybody? You didn't, did you?"

"So what if I didn't? Why are you asking me all these questions?"

"Don't you know? I'm trying to get to know the famous Maddy Brown. The famous liar, the famous phony, the—"

"Why are you saying such horrible things?"

"Because I'm seeing the real you for the first time, Maddy!" I turned and started down the hill, my heart almost exploding in my chest. "And you know why my eyesight's suddenly so good?"

"No, *why?*" she yelled after me, trying to sound smart-alecky, which is hard to do when your voice is shaking.

I threw it back over my shoulder at her.

"Because I'm seeing you through *Vermont eyes!*"

Okay, scratch Maddy Brown. *But at least you told her off.*

Camilla was right. She's a phony.

She used me. She probably never liked me even a little bit and was laughing behind my back the whole time with Jillie and the others.

So what? At least now I know the truth.

And I will be stronger for it—won't I?

I chanted the above silently to myself all the way home on the bus, but it didn't help one bit. I felt absolutely miserable.

And I continued to feel miserable as I scurried through the halls the next couple of days, trying to avoid just about everyone in the school because I was sure they were whispering about me. By Thursday my paranoia—grapefruit-size to begin with—was the size of the Goodyear blimp and I was absolutely exhausted.

Needless to say, I hadn't told anyone what had happened at Maddy's house. Sometimes, I wanted to tell *everybody.* In fact, in one of my more insane moments I actually considered inserting a notice into "Daily Doings" to be read over the public address system. It would say something like:

This is to warn all students, but most especially those in junior high, to be alert and on guard to any false promises, statements, or claims made by Madison Brown, a seventh grade student newly transferred from New York City and currently enrolled in Homeroom 201. This person has no interest in our school or community, and is here only under duress. She has never, repeat *never*, made any movie except one "ABC Afterschool Special," and most assuredly wouldn't know Kevin Costner if she fell over him at the bus stop. In short, she is a liar, a cheat, and maybe most important, a very conceited person who gives lousy beauty tips.

I thought it might fit nicely sandwiched between the pitch to buy the yearbook and the warning about overdue library books.

But truthfully, since *I'd* been the number-one fool, most of the time I didn't really want anyone to know. And the sad thing is, I really didn't have anyone to *tell* since I was currently at war with half the town.

Besides Madison Brown, I wasn't on speaking terms with Camilla Moss—even though she tried to be friendly—because just when I was beginning to like her, to feel that maybe here was a kindred spirit that understood how I felt, she had gone behind my back and asked my mom to be a chaperone. I know I was right there when she did it, but still it was behind my back.

And of course, I wasn't on speaking terms with my mother since we'd had that argument about the Halloween dance.

So who else would I want to tell? Certainly not the Kirby twins, even though I had plenty of opportunity since I was back sitting with them at lunchtime.

Thursday evening, after we'd finished another silent supper, I went in to study for the earth science test that I was sure I was going to fail the next day. (My life was really going great on all burners—you know the feeling?) Anyway, I'd been staring at the map on page 52 for almost an hour when suddenly Paisley came rushing into my room out of breath.

"Come on, we're going to be late!" She must have noticed the confused look on my face, because she said brusquely, "The planning board meeting? We have to be there for the Mosses. I almost forgot all about it!"

"I'm not going."

"Of course you're going. I promised Mrs. Moss we'd be there."

"Well, I won't be."

You made a fool of yourself last week; I am not going to go there and be humiliated again!

I knew all these terrible feelings had been building inside me, like poison gas filling up a house, but now they were trying to get loose—to crawl out a window or sneak up the chimney and escape before I blew up inside.

"Don't *ever* speak to me in that tone of voice,

Holly," my mother said calmly, in the same voice she used to correct my manners.

"I have to study. I have a test tomorrow," I said, figuring here was the argument that no mother could brush aside. But Paisley had a different set of priorities from other mothers. How could I have forgotten that?

"This is more important than learning about some stupid earthquake. Anyway, we won't be gone long. Since it was tabled last week, the Moss thing will be first on the agenda."

I stared down at the map trying to think of some excuse that would make her leave me alone.

"I don't feel very well," I said, knowing how lame it sounded.

"I thought you and Camilla had become friends. You know, she doesn't have anyone else in this town. This is the least you can do for her."

"We're not ..." I swallowed hard, realizing with horror that I was on the verge of tears. I had started to say "We're not friends," but the words stuck in my throat as Kelly Kirby's words came back to me: "We'll always accept you, even without Linda."

In spite of who you are.

Maybe Camilla and I *weren't* friends yet. Maybe we never would be. But suddenly, I knew that if I said those words I'd be closing that door forever.

I grabbed my jacket while my mother went out to start up the van. As we made our way down to the center of town I stole a glance at her. It was amazing how straight and righteous Paisley could be sometimes.

The meeting hall wasn't nearly as crowded as the week before. At first I felt a flood of relief, but the scant turnout made it easier to see who *was* there and my heart sank.

Kelly and Kim were standing up in the front of the room, near where they'd been the last time. And Camilla and her mother were across from them, just as before. But in the second row I spied Joey Whitelaw (he was always so easy to spot!) and Gina with her mother—and on the other side of her, Maddy Brown.

Kelly gave me a worried look as we came in, knitting her forehead together in a true Kirby frown. Then she slipped away from her father and came over to us. She smiled sweetly at my mother, and then pulling me aside by the sleeve of my jacket, she muttered, "What are you doing here? I thought we agreed that you wouldn't let your mother come again!"

I swallowed hard. I had forgotten about that.

"I couldn't stop her," I said, hearing myself stammer as if I'd been caught by the principal doing something wrong.

Kelly hurled a look of disgust at me and went back to sit down with her folks. And as she did, Camilla turned around. She looked relieved when she saw me; she smiled and gave me a little wave. But I pretended not to see.

There were folding chairs along the wall near the front, put there for times when the crowd was so large that people had to stand two deep near the door. Now Paisley was nudging me to sit there.

I looked at her and shook my head. We'd be sitting practically in everyone's lap! Didn't she understand, I wanted to hide! I wanted to sit out in the lobby!

"We'll be able to slip out easier from here," she whispered. Just then the clerk banged the gavel to bring the meeting to order, so we sat down quickly.

"First on the agenda, we have to dispose of this special-use permit requested by Ernestine Moss. We had a few opinions expressed last week, but as I'm sure you're aware, there are pretty hard-and-fast rules about this sort of thing, and we can't be swayed just by speeches. It's not a popularity contest. Or a matter in which we let personalities get involved." I began to feel relieved. It sounded as if Camilla's mother was going to win, and Kelly and her family would be taught a lesson. But then he said, "However, in this case there seems to be a general consensus of opinion that this would establish a very bad precedent. And, while keenly aware that we have here an ... unfortunate ... aspect to the family situation, we must do what is right for the greater good of the community and abide by the letter of the law. Therefore, the Moss application as submitted is denied."

A murmur went through the room and a few people even began to clap, and I could see a smug smile beginning to spread across Kelly's face. But then the gavel came down again and he continued. "However, this board wants to be fair and we would be agreeable to some sort of compromise here if one of our established merchants would be willing to, let us say, be a guarantor of this endeavor."

They were hypocrites, that's what they were! Trying to save face—throwing the Mosses a bone, so they couldn't say there was any prejudice or meanness involved. They already knew the mood of the community. Did they really think somebody like Mr. Kirby was suddenly going to reach out and give them a helping hand?

I felt it even before I saw it. Paisley's hand went up and in a moment she was on her feet.

"Your honor," she began.

"Your name, please," the clerk said in his monotonous voice.

"Oh, for God's sake, Pete, you know who I am," she muttered. Then, "Paisley Gerard of 12 Ridge Road, and *I'll* give the guarantee!"

Faces had turned in our direction and I tried not to see, as usual. But then I glanced up and I saw one face and it was like someone had stabbed me, that's how sharp it felt. Mrs. Moss was holding back tears, you could tell, and she was biting her lip and I just knew, even without being close by, that she was barely breathing.

"I'll guarantee," Paisley repeated. "Mrs. Moss and I are going to be partners. Isn't that right, Ernestine? So you don't have to bother about the variance, she can work out of Paisley's Place."

My face was flushed so hot I thought I was going to explode. I looked at the faces around me and some looked relieved and some looked annoyed, and then I saw Camilla's face and it was shining like a new penny. Next to her, for the first time, I saw Nancy smile.

"Is there anyone else who wishes to comment on this suggestion or to second this motion?"

There was a hush in the room as if each person there was holding his breath and I knew that nobody else was going to come forward; they were going to let Paisley stand alone on the fringe of the room, just like she'd always stood alone on the fringe of the town. Maybe someone agreeing was just a formality—but maybe it was the kind of thing that mattered at a time like this.

I will never remember how it happened. Honestly. But the next thing I knew I was on my feet.

"Holly Gerard, and I live at 12 Ridge Road, too, your honor, and I'm ... I'm a student at Old MacIntosh Junior/Senior High School." I had to stop to catch my breath because now that I was standing and everyone was staring at me my mind was going blank and I could hardly breathe. "I ... I would just like to say that I'm glad the Mosses can stay in town. I think they'll be an asset and I think you're to be congratulated, sir. I just wanted you to know that. Oh, and I *second* the motion!"

I sat down then, and though *I* don't remember hearing it, later on Paisley told me that some of the people in the hall gave me a round of applause. But that wasn't important. The important thing was the way I felt. It took a few minutes, because you can imagine how much I was shaking, but finally I raised my head and looked at some of the people. I figured they'd all be glowering at me and even snarling, maybe. But you know what? I think they must have had other business to take care of and other things on their mind, because they weren't staring at all. Except for Kelly Kirby. But I just stared right back at her and I felt better in that moment than I could ever remember feeling. Even when Linda was around.

And you know something else? Remember that cramped, tight feeling I always get? It was all gone.

J would like to report that I never got that cramped, tight feeling again, but if I did I'd be lying and I don't do that anymore. But I am working on looking at things in a different way—I was beginning to feel less hysterical about the Halloween dance, for instance—and so I don't get it as much. It's weird: All my life I've hated having people stare at us or talk about us, but the minute I got up and acted as crazy as my mother, I felt better, stronger, you know? I think all of a sudden I realized, What were they going to do, shoot me? No, what they were going to do was stare at me the way Kelly Kirby did, and I had found out how easy it was to return fire. When I stared back at her, *she* was the one who looked away.

The morning after the meeting I was prepared for the worst when I got on the bus and, sure enough, the seat next to Kelly was already taken. So I saved a seat for Camilla and I think that arrangement's going to be permanent. And you know what? Camilla and I got just as many hi's as I used to when I sat next to Kelly. (Of course I counted them. I'm not *that* secure yet.)

*   *   *

As if my mother sensed the changes that were happening inside me, and the different way I was trying to look at things, one night she started talking over the pot-au-feu. She was using a different voice, as if she was really on earth for a change, so I paid attention.

"Do you know how proud I was of you, when you stood up at the town meeting?" Did I *know*. She ranted and raved and gushed and beamed all the way home and for two days afterward. "Well, I just want to be sure that you're not still worried about me being at the Halloween dance," she said softly.

"Worry? *Me?*"

"Yeah, you. Because it's next Saturday night, and I thought we'd better start working on what we're going to wear."

"Oh, right," I said, pretending to concentrate on chewing my food one hundred times a bite.

"I know you don't think I'm aware of your feelings," she went on. All of a sudden, she was a mind reader! "And in a way, you're right. I've been pretty obtuse about some things." I must have given her a blank look then, because she said "insensitive" and not just "look it up" the way she usually does.

"That's okay," I said, finding my voice.

"I just want to say, I tried to be the kind of mother I wish I'd had." I looked across at her. "They didn't have those horrible little ducks in my day, but if they had, your grandmother would have had them all over the house."

141

"Really?"

"Really. I mean, she outbaked Linda's mother, and I couldn't go to school without tripping over her. You think you see a lot of Mrs. Barnes? Well, my mother chaired every damn committee and had her hand in everything." Here she gave a little laugh, like she was enjoying a private joke. "And the hand always had a white glove on it," she added.

"I don't remember Grandma too well."

"I know you don't. She died too soon." She let out a big sigh. "I don't think I realized until now how much I miss her. It's no fun rebelling when there's nothing to rebel against, you know?" I didn't know, so I just stayed quiet. "What I wanted to say is, I know you've been—God, how I hate saying this—embarrassed by your mother, but I thought it was just your age. But maybe I didn't see because I didn't want to see."

"That's okay," I said again, staring down at my plate. I had this gigantic lump in my throat. Was there going to be a punch line? Was she going to go into the other room and come out in some outlandish costume for the dance?

"I just wanted you to know that I will wear whatever you want me to wear to the dance."

"You will?"

"Of course." But then, Paisley being Paisley, there *was* a punch line. "Just let me know in advance," she added, "because if it's a tweed suit, it's gonna take me a little time to get it together."

We laughed then, but it was a load off my mind

142

and I asked Camilla about it the next day. She said Mr. Harper was coming as a clown, and Miss Boswell as a witch.

"So why doesn't your mom come as a gypsy?"

"Is that supposed to be funny?"

"No, really! Think about it: She has all those funky clothes, why not go with it? What do *you* want her to come as, a *nurse?*"

I thought about it and Camilla was right, as usual. *You gotta make it work for you.* This might be the one occasion when Paisley's "look" wouldn't be out of place.

When I told her she seemed relieved, and we put together an outfit that was only a little more creative than what she wore to shop at Kirby's. We even had fun, I've got to admit, trying on the different skirts, and layering them to get just the right effect. I felt it was very important that she look like a genuine gypsy and not just like Paisley going out to get the mail. But she must have thought of this, too, because she was the one who came up with a solution.

"Look," she said, coming out of her bedroom and holding out a small crystal globe. She lifted the hem of her skirt and began trying to shine it up.

"What's that?" I asked.

"My crystal ball! You know. I've told you how I used to tell fortunes down in Greenwich Village."

"I guess I didn't realize it was real, honest-to-God fortune-telling."

"Well, I don't know about the honest-to-God

143

part, but I gave it my best shot. It's just a thought, mind you, but it seems to me that girls your age just love to have their fortunes told. But, of course, I won't make a move without your permission."

"Honest?"

"Honest."

Once we had Paisley put together, we had to get to work on my outfit. Camilla had taken my favorite dress, the ruby red one, but there was another favorite of mine that nobody had taken because the hem was ripped. It was ivory satin, with spangles and sequins all over the top. It was absolutely gorgeous and Paisley sat up one night and sewed the hem, and then we teamed it with a feather thing for my hair and she showed me how to wear my stockings rolled around my knees, flapper style. Of course, once I put it on, I realized there was another reason why none of the other kids had picked it. It weighed a ton. Between the weight of the dress and all the makeup Paisley made me wear, and the stockings that kept slipping down around my ankles, it was not going to be the most comfortable night of my life. But when I stood real still and posed in front of the mirror, I looked terrific.

When we got to school on Saturday night and I saw Mr. Harper made up as a clown and Miss Boswell dressed as a witch, I realized that all the chaperones were really just coming as their true selves and that made me stop worrying so much about Paisley.

Anyway, I had my hands full just trying to keep the stockings up.

We had to be there early, so now as I stood holding up the wall waiting for the dance to begin, I was really sorry I hadn't thought to tell Camilla we'd pick her up. She was the only friend that I was sure of tonight, and even though I was trying to be a whole new person, every once in a while the old me would slip back, as if it had just been hiding behind a Halloween mask.

I looked around at what Gina and her crew had done in the way of Halloween decorations. Obviously she hates anything that the rest of us would think of as appropriate for the occasion, and instead was very big on being "different." Instead of pumpkins, she had oranges on the table, and she had draped black material everywhere, making the gym not scary or spooky but just dark and depressing, like a convention of undertakers were having a luau.

I practiced my positive thinking while I waited: *I am popular, I am strong, I don't care what anybody thinks.*

This worked really well as long as I was by myself. But when Maddy and Gina walked through the door with Kelly and Kim, I thought I'd faint. They weren't wearing the flapper dresses! Gina was dressed like a scarecrow, the twins as Mickey and Minnie, and Maddy as—who else? Catwoman. It wasn't hard to figure out what message they were sending. I was out, O-U-T, and they wouldn't be caught dead in costumes from Paisley's Place. Jillie wasn't with them, but it was pretty clear that when she did arrive (with Bobby on a leash, as usual) she'd be wearing something else too.

It was almost eight-thirty before Camilla came bounding through the door.

"Sorry! I couldn't get my mom off the phone long enough to drive me over here."

"I am *so* glad you're here!" I said, relief flooding through me. And it was only when I heard those words out loud that I realized how true they were. I was so comfortable with Camilla, and I don't think it was only because she also had—as Kelly had so delicately put it—a bad family situation. I think we just fit, you know? She's braver than I am about a lot of things, and obviously much more mature, but I make her laugh and that's important because thinking as much as Camilla does can really get a person down. Anyway, I'm not saying we'll still be friends when we're old ladies or even that we'll go to each other's weddings. All I'm sure of is that as I stood there sweating in my fifty-pound costume, with stockings around my ankles and makeup sticking to my face like pizza, I was really glad to see her.

I poked her arm and nodded over to where the others were standing in a huddle.

"Ah, a revolt," she said. "Well, that's good. This way you and I will stand out. You look sensational, by the way."

"So do you!" I said, almost cracking heads with her as I bent once more to jerk up the stockings.

"I'm starved. Have you been over to the snacks yet?" she asked.

"No, you want to?"

"Sure. It'll give us something to do. I have a feeling the only one who's going to ask me to dance is you, and that doesn't get me all excited."

I giggled as we made our way through the thickening crowd.

The band was called the Electric Erasers and consisted of four seniors who'd started playing at parties last year. They were really good. So good that we couldn't hear anything we said, so we contented ourselves with devouring all the chips and dip. It was so nice not having somebody standing over me counting the potato chips and explaining in gory detail how each one would ultimately lead to a small, thoroughly disgusting explosion somewhere on my face.

"Uh-oh," Camilla said, taking a peek over my shoulder.

"What's the matter?" I said, as I felt the crunch of someone squeezing in right next to us.

"Hey, Holly!" Joey Whitelaw was yelling to be heard over the din. "I been meanin' to tell you, you were *great* the other night." I stared at him dumbly. "You know, AT THE MEETING?"

The band had stopped and the last three words exploded in the sudden silence.

"Oh," I said, embarrassed. "Thank you."

Maddy slipped her hand through his arm. "Come on, let's dance," she purred.

"They're taking a break."

"That's all right, we'll go wait for them to start up again!"

147

"Wait a minute, I want to get somethin' to eat."

"You don't want any of that," she said, wrinkling her cute little nose.

He looked at her as if she were out of her mind.

"You crazy? Of course I do!"

Paisley came drifting toward us then, slowly twirling her crystal ball.

"What do you think? I thought I'd set up shop out in the hall. This doesn't seem like such a wild bunch; those other two can hold down the fort."

I took a deep breath. "I don't know," I said. What had seemed like a good idea when everybody was wearing dresses from Paisley's Place seemed stupid now that they'd dumped us.

"How *tack-y*," Maddy said, mouthing the words to Joey in a stage whisper that she knew I could hear. But just as she said it, there was a squeal behind me.

"I just *heard!* Can we start with the fortunes now?"

Jillie had picked the slinky black crepe shift with the fringed hem and the scoop neckline, and now it looked sensational with a "diamond" tiara sitting on top of the blonde curls she'd managed for the occasion. Bobby was supposed to be her Roaring Twenties date, I was told, but I must say he looked more like Count Dracula with his hair slicked back and wearing a tuxedo that was two sizes too big for him.

Maddy removed her hand from Joey and leaned over to Jillie, pretending to get a cracker.

148

"I thought you weren't going to wear it," she said in a singsong voice. "It's probably *diseased.*"

"Oh, that's so dumb! Anyway, I never agreed—"

"Well, we all did."

"Who's we all?" Jillie said, sounding annoyed. I wasn't sure if it was intentional or not, but she seemed to be imitating Maddy's drawl.

"Everyone. Everyone in my—"

"In your what, your *fan* club?" Jillie said, nudging Bobby, and they both laughed and then Joey let out a snort (did I mention that he laughs like a really cheerful goat?), which made Madison Brown livid.

"I should have *known.* You're all hopeless, I don't know why I even tried!"

This outburst only made everyone laugh even more.

"Oh Maddy, you're such a *ham!*" Jillie said, laughing gaily. But I noticed she never let go of Bobby's arm.

My mother had slipped away while all this was going on, and now Jillie looked around.

"Where'd she go?" she asked.

"Out in the hall, I guess."

"Well, let's go catch her. I just love having my fortune told, don't you? You know your mom is so *neat.* Can you imagine my mother in a costume? She'd rather die. That whole school board is such a bunch of nerds!"

I found myself nodding sympathetically. Since the band had started up again that's all I could do.

Paisley told so many fortunes that I thought

149

she'd drop before the night was over. And both Camilla and I noticed that a subtle shift had begun. Maddy Brown was out on the ice floe with Kelly, Kim, and Gina, while Jillie giggled with us as if we were old friends.

But the rift wasn't really complete until the end of the evening. As the Electric Erasers swung into the slow last number, Jamie Miller asked Camilla to dance and I was really happy for her. Honest. Then I felt a hand on my arm and I was even happier for *me*.

And he wasn't too tall at all.

Just when I was learning to think of my mother as exotic, interesting, and a free spirit, instead of eccentric, weird, and a nut, she had to go and have a midlife crisis.

It started with Ernestine. They're both really excited about their partnership, but remember the way I told you Mrs. Moss *looked* that first day she was in the shop? Really bewildered and nervous? Well, she looked that way again when she came over to plan the new setup with Paisley, and the next day she showed up with a car full of cleaning supplies. Paisley seemed a little bewildered at first, but after Camilla's mother explained that it would be good for the environment she pitched right in, and by the time we'd all spent one entire weekend on our hands and knees, Paisley's Place was spotless, and later on I actually caught my mother putting something away in a *drawer.*

I think the new shop is going to be good for both of them. Since the stock they're importing is really unusual, my mom doesn't feel as if she's selling out to the Establishment. And at the same time, it seems to have had a beneficial effect on her wardrobe. The other day I saw her pull a simple plaid shirt out of a pile and team it with a pair of jeans, giving herself an almost preppy image. But then as an afterthought she topped it off with a Mexican shawl, perhaps remembering that the new place *is* going to be called Paisley International.

We're getting to be one big, happy, if unbalanced, family. Mr. Moss was home one weekend on a furlough and we all went out to dinner together. And Camilla was right. He *is* a nice man, and when he comes home for good next month I think I'm going to be almost as glad to have him around as Camilla and Nancy.

Speaking of Nancy, she's doing better too. We take her with us to the mall, and to the library, and she's not feeling so lonely anymore. She's even beginning to make a few friends of her own.

The lunchroom setup has switched around: Camilla and I usually sit together at the table against the wall, but sometimes we join Jillie's table—when they beg us—just so they won't think we're antisocial.

And Maddy Brown is hanging out almost exclusively with Kelly and Kim now, although it seems to me she's showing a marked preference for Kim.

We were snacking at Camilla's house one day after school (it was the day we had both gotten invitations to Jillie's birthday party) and I was feeling so good that without thinking I said, "Isn't it *great* how everybody accepts you now?" She looked at me kind of funny so I quickly added, "Oh, I

152

mean *both* of us—in spite of, you know, who we are."

She looked at me even funnier. "What are you talking about? I don't want people to like me in spite of who I am—are you nuts?"

"What do you mean?"

"That is so insulting, Holly. Like they're doing us a favor? That's the way Kelly Kirby treated you! 'Don't forget to be grateful that I allow you to live on the same planet.' No one should like you 'in spite of.' " I didn't say anything, but she must have known what I was thinking, because she said, "Linda was that way, too, wasn't she?"

"Oh, no!" I said quickly. Then I added, "Well, maybe just a little bit. But I'm sorry, Camilla. Maybe being in and accepted isn't important to you, but it still is to me."

"Of course it's important. I want people to like me, and they will. But because of who I am, not in spite of." Sometimes having Camilla for a best friend was absolutely exhausting. "You don't get it, do you?" she said, seeing the expression on my face.

"Not really," I had to admit, taking another potato chip.

But maybe I'm beginning to.

About the Author

"I'm sure that my love for 'browsing' partly inspired this story," says author Sheila Hayes. "On family ski trips to Vermont, when everybody else hit the slopes, I'd hit the antique shops—the more cluttered, the better!"

Ms. Hayes was born and raised in New York City, where she attended Marymount Manhattan College and Columbia University. She has published seven other books for young readers. She and her husband live in Briarcliff Manor, New York. They have three grown daughters.

JF Hayes
Hayes, Sheila.
The tinker's daughter